# The Path to You - Special Edition

## The Wilder Brothers
### Book 3

Carrie Ann Ryan

# THE PATH TO YOU

## A WILDER BROTHERS NOVEL

By
Carrie Ann Ryan

The Path to You - Special Edition
A Wilder Brothers Novel
By: Carrie Ann Ryan
© 2022 Carrie Ann Ryan
Paperback ISBN 978-1-63695-263-5

Cover Art by Sweet N Spicy Designs

# Praise for Carrie Ann Ryan

"Count on Carrie Ann Ryan for emotional, sexy, character driven stories that capture your heart!" – Carly Phillips, NY Times bestselling author

"Carrie Ann Ryan's romances are my newest addiction! The emotion in her books captures me from the very beginning. The hope and healing hold me close until the end. These love stories will simply sweep you away." ~ NYT Bestselling Author Deveny Perry

"Carrie Ann Ryan writes the perfect balance of sweet and heat ensuring every story feeds the soul." - Audrey Carlan, #1 New York Times Bestselling Author

"Carrie Ann Ryan never fails to draw readers in with passion, raw sensuality, and characters that pop off the page. Any book by Carrie Ann is an absolute treat." – New York Times Bestselling Author J. Kenner

"Carrie Ann Ryan knows how to pull your heartstrings and make your pulse pound! Her wonderful Redwood Pack series will draw you in and keep you reading long into the night. I can't wait to see what comes next with the new generation, the Talons. Keep them coming, Carrie Ann!" –Lara Adrian, New York Times bestselling author of CRAVE THE NIGHT

"With snarky humor, sizzling love scenes, and brilliant, imaginative worldbuilding, The Dante's Circle series reads as if Carrie Ann Ryan peeked at my personal wish list!" – NYT Bestselling Author, Larissa Ione

"Carrie Ann Ryan writes sexy shifters in a world full of passionate happily-ever-afters." – *New York Times* Bestselling Author Vivian Arend

"Carrie Ann's books are sexy with characters you can't help but love from page one. They are heat and heart blended to perfection." *New York Times* Bestselling Author Jayne Rylon

Carrie Ann Ryan's books are wickedly funny and deliciously hot, with plenty of twists to keep you guessing. They'll keep you up all night!" USA Today Bestselling Author Cari Quinn

"Once again, Carrie Ann Ryan knocks the Dante's Circle series out of the park. The queen of hot, sexy, enthralling paranormal romance, Carrie Ann is an author not to miss!" *New York Times* bestselling Author Marie Harte

# THE PATH TO YOU

The Wilder Brothers from NYT Bestselling Author Carrie Ann Ryan continues with a second chance romance that brings Everett Wilder to his knees.

The moment I saw Bethany Cole, I knew she was not only out of my league, but in a whole different world.

Only I didn't realize I'd met her before.

An explosion stole part of my past, including the first time I'd seen her pretty face.

Now she's an A-list celebrity.

And I'm just a Wilder.

But when her boyfriend cheats on her, Bethany needs a safe place to hide from the paparazzi.

The Wilder's Retreat seems like the perfect escape.

Only every time we see each other it's hard to remember we come from two different worlds.

And that the danger that follows her is only the beginning.

# Chapter One

Bethany

"You monster! You think I'm the one that broke everything? You're the one that stands out on your balcony over the world you think you've created. You have used the blood, sweat, and tears of those you hate in order to get where you are. And yet *I'm* the monster for turning you in? Why can't you look in the mirror and see who the true horror is?"

The man turned to me, his eyes narrowed, death in his gaze. "I wouldn't look in the mirror. I just have to kill you, and there will be nothing left to stand in my way."

He moved towards me, hands outstretched, but I stood my ground, knowing I was stronger than him. Even if it broke me.

"Cut!" the director called out, and I rolled my shoulders back and smiled up at Jackson.

"How did that feel?" I asked, and he ran his hand over his mouth, his dark gaze softening, that stern jaw melting into a wicked smile.

"It feels like we got it, but let's see what the director says."

We turned to Sanchez, who stared at his notes in front of him and nodded. "That's good enough for today. Decent job, both of you."

Then he turned on his heel and walked out with the writer at his side, both of them mumbling something to the other. The dozens of other people on set moved as a unit, each with a particular job, just like they'd done a thousand times before.

I looked over at Jackson and held back a smile.

A decent job in Sanchez's eyes was Oscar-worthy in anyone else's. I counted that as a blessing, considering the man didn't know how to give praise and was never happy. I liked working with him but was glad I had only one more day of shooting. This film had been exhausting, with the training, stunts, last-minute changes to the script, and constant worry over outside forces I couldn't control.

But I was already proud of the work I'd done.

That was what I did.

I was Bethany Cole, Golden Globe, Emmy, and SAG award-winning actress, who also happened to be the lead in an upcoming superhero film.

My lips twitched as I thought about it. I listened to Jackson as he went over notes for the day.

"You still have another week?" I asked, looking over at my costar and leading man.

He nodded. "I do. I can't wait get home to Max and the kids. This has been a long shoot, and since our oldest is starting kindergarten, we didn't want them to travel as much once the school year started. It's been a little weird doing nearly an entire movie without them in my trailer during the day waiting for me to finish."

"So, they flew back up to Idaho?" I asked.

Jackson nodded. "Yes, I thought I mentioned that." He frowned. "Didn't I?"

I shook my head. "No, you just said at home. But I understand. The kids have a better chance of a normal life up there, with good schools, rather than living that LA life."

"Tell me about it. We're going to try this and see how it

goes. My schedule isn't as busy as it once was. I know that some actors call that the death knell, but to me, it just means I did something right in my past so that I can look to my future." He let out a breath and rolled his shoulders back. He was no longer the Devil of Manhattan but instead an Oscar-award-winning actor who was finally settling down with his husband of five years and their two children. He was kinder than the man he'd been portraying for the past few weeks—a murderer on a killing spree.

I liked Jackson; he was one of the most brilliant actors of our generation. I was only a little jealous that he seemed to have his life in order when I was still scrambling to figure out mine. Even if the headlines thought I was well on my way into that celebrity future of stardom, multiple Oscars, and marriage with another leading man.

That reminded me, that I needed to text Dallas and tell him I would be on my way home soon, but maybe I would just do it later. It wasn't like we lived together. I could see him tomorrow. I'd been up early, and it *had* been a long day. I wanted to take a bath, have a glass of wine, and go over my next script. I had a months-long break before I had to start my next movie, and I could perhaps fit in something else, depending on what my agent thought. I wasn't sure I could take a break. Because if I did, Hollywood could forget about me.

They tended to do that pretty quickly when you were heading to your dotage.

And considering I was twenty-five, I was well on my way to being ancient in this business.

I wasn't a fan of where my thoughts had turned, so I pushed those from my mind.

I went back to my trailer, laughed with my team and makeup artists as we changed me from the strong, competent, and slightly insane character I was playing back into just Bethany.

I pulled my hair back into a messy bun, slid on oversized sunglasses, and stared at the white T-shirt and skinny jeans I wore.

"Not too bad after a long day," I said after a moment.

My assistant, Tonya, smiled. "Not bad at all. Do you want me to order you dinner and call Trace and the driver?"

Trace was my head of security, and we made a good team.

"No, I'm fine. I'm heading home. I'll see you tomorrow for the last day, though. And I know we have a few things to do before you get a break."

Tonya rolled her eyes. "We both know that neither of us knows how to take breaks."

"That is true." I laughed and headed out to my car. I made the drive home, a little tired and grateful for the iced coffee that Tonya had got for me so I wouldn't have to head to the busy coffee shop on the corner. I liked doing things on my own, but since people knew precisely where we were shooting, it was filled with paparazzi and people who wanted my time. I loved my fans and would do anything for them, but I also needed a minute to breathe after a long day of filming, especially when it was as emotional as today had been.

I lived a little over an hour from where the shoot was taking place, though sometimes with traffic it turned into three hours. Those days it was a hassle, so I was grateful that it only took an hour and a half to get home. I could have used the studio-assigned driver, but I just wanted time alone. I couldn't wait to take the night off just to breathe, and then I could read some scripts and get ready for those two large back-to-back movies that I had that would take a lot out of me emotionally and physically. Maybe I would take a break as my agent suggested, or maybe I would find an indie project in the middle. I didn't know, but I would figure out something. Right before this movie started, I had taken a three-week trip to work with my favorite charities, so maybe I would return to that—one where I didn't have cameras in my face, documenting everything that I did.

I was blessed with my job, with the work that I was getting, with the praise from my fellow actors and industry professionals. But I always knew I had to give back.

After all, I was only here because of state scholarships and charities when I was younger, barely able to make it through the day after losing my mom, then my dad.

I pulled in past the security station of the neighborhood, waved at Tom, the guard on duty, and headed towards my house on the back lot. I hadn't always lived in a place like this. The necessary security and high walls. I wasn't an LA girl by birth or even by choice really.

But after my fourth movie had broken records and people had started to know my name, I needed to keep people away from my home.

Having that kind woman break into my bathroom, just to say hello to me and make sure that I was using the right shampoo for my hair, scared me enough to spend the money on a larger house. Apparently, it was just the way it was in my new life, but sometimes I missed my shabby apartment with four deadbolts and a rickety window.

I pulled into my garage and noticed that Dallas's car was also parked in my guest spot.

That didn't mean he was here. He had multiple cars and a driver with his producer's car service. He rarely drove these days unless he wanted to show off one of his beauties, preferring to sit in the back and have people drive him about. I wasn't a huge fan of driving myself, especially in LA traffic, but after a long day when I was the focus of everybody's attention, I wanted to be alone. Hence driving myself home.

I hadn't thought Dallas would be here today, and I wasn't sure I was up to dealing with my boyfriend.

That thought made me pause. Dallas was my boyfriend. Our agents had set us up because of publicity, but then we had truly started to date. Most of the world thought we were well on our way to being married, and half of them thought I was already pregnant.

Mainly because, God forbid, I didn't starve myself like they wanted me to. I dealt with the constant articles on my weight, my health, and my love life. I just wanted some time alone today and wasn't in the mood to deal with Dallas and his moods. And he was always in a mood. Considering that he was about to start a major superhero movie alongside me, he was living his best life. People were coming to him now instead of him going to them. He wanted the accolades I had, and more. He deserved them, he was a great actor, but he was also lazy, egotistical, and that bothered me.

I rubbed my temple, wondering why I was even still dating him.

I loved him.

And he was stressed, and I could live through that as long as we had each other.

Noise from the TV sounded from my office, and I frowned, wondering why Dallas was in there. He liked being in there sometimes to look at my awards. My manager had built an entire shelf to house them, doing his best not to leave a space for an Oscar. One did not leave room for awards. One made space for them after, especially if you wanted to make sure that you didn't jinx yourself.

While I was proud of my accomplishments, I also wasn't sure I liked looking at them every time I was in there because the pressure and memories from each one compounded on each other.

Dallas was here, maybe he would want to make a nice dinner at home. We could just relax.

Dallas was good at relaxing.

"Yes, right there. Do it. Yes. Harder. You know what I like, baby."

I frowned, tension shooting up my spine as that voice hit my ears. I knew that voice.

Maybe I was just imagining things.

Because I didn't think it was coming from the TV anymore.

When I turned towards my office, the scripts in my hands dropped to the floor. I stared as my boyfriend, Dallas Huntington, railed his mediocre cock into Cassandra Fox, the media's darling and my rival, at least according to the tabloids.

Neither of them saw me, both angled so that they were facing each other, all their attention on one another as he continued fucking her on top of my desk. My awards shone behind her, the light on in the cabinet, so it looked like she was surrounded by a halo of trophies.

She arched her head back, her perfect round breasts bouncing with each thrust.

Dallas groaned, flexing his ass, one that he worked on for countless hours to keep toned, as he banged the woman I truly hated in my office.

"Are you kidding me?" I asked, my voice sharper than I intended. I hadn't meant to say anything because I wasn't sure what I was supposed to say.

Dallas continued to move, thrusting harder, as he looked over his shoulder and winked. "Be right with you, baby."

"Excuse me?" I marched forward and turned off the light behind them, shaking my head. "There's no need to waste electricity. I'm not sure why you are fucking in front of my bookshelf in my office anyway."

I didn't know why I was making a big deal about that.

Because he was still deep inside her, both of them now frozen.

Cassandra pouted, then slid her hand over her clit. "You are such a bitch. I was almost done, Bethany. Hell."

Dallas sighed, then pulled out of her, and I added getting myself checked out to the list because he wasn't wearing a condom. I visibly shuddered, then glared at the two of them.

"Are you kidding me right now?" I asked again. Because if I kept worrying about my office, its cleanliness, anything else, I wouldn't feel that step off the trail as it stabbed into me repeatedly. As my life felt like nothing made sense, and I wanted to scream or throw up, I wondered why he was cheating on me. In my own house. In my office.

"Stop making a big deal," Cassandra waved it off as she hopped off the desk with her perfect athletic grace and slid her dress back on.

Dallas rolled his eyes and stuffed himself back into his pants. "Why are you freaking out? What the hell is wrong with you?"

"Why am I freaking out." I said very calmly. As calmly as I could make it. "Because you were screwing another woman in my house, in my office. How long has this been going on? What do you think you were doing?"

"Oh, stop it, Bethany. You knew he was with me, too. You know the tabloids love putting us against each other. I've been *against Dallas* this whole time." As she said it, she winked as if she was making a joke.

I just stood there, slack-jawed, anger and hurt rolling over me. "You were cheating on me. This whole time?"

"It's not cheating if it's a full relationship," Dallas said.

He was delusional. "No. That's not how any of this works. Get the fuck out of my house."

"Whatever. I was done anyway. Not with you, baby," he swooned over to Cassandra. Then he looked at me. "You're never a good lay. Honestly, it was fun while it lasted, but I'm tired now. Dealing with you and your drama is just exhausting. So, it's over."

"Do you think you're the one breaking up with me? Because no, that's not how this is going to work. You're cheating on me, so you get out of my house. It's over."

"Whatever you say, baby. Just know if you bring this out to the press, I'll crucify you."

I froze, my mind whirling in a thousand different directions as I tried to keep up. "Excuse me?"

"I know things about you, darling. Things that would make anyone's skin crawl. You think you're Hollywood's darling? I don't think so. They're going to know the real you. So, if you say anything about me? Anything about us, about Cassandra? I'll ruin you. You're just so you. A woman that's reached her peak. Past her prime. You're old, and soon the scripts are going to stop coming for you. They only want you now because they can use you. Just like I did. You are one bad tabloid away from nothing. Remember that, because I'll have forever in this business. You're just a woman. So don't mess with me."

He pushed past me, elbowing me in the gut as he did so, and I whirled, ready to lash out, but Cassandra stood there, phone in her hand.

"Do it. Hit him because I'm the one that's going to win here. I always do."

Then she winked, whirled on her high heels, and sauntered out of my house, as if she hadn't just been banging my boyfriend in my office.

I pulled out my phone, my eyes wide as my heart raced. There was a metallic taste in my mouth, and I told myself I needed to stop panicking. I need to be calm about this.

Because everything just got messy. So damn messy.

Trace picked up on the first ring. "I think something bad just happened."

And that was the understatement of understatements.

---

Word of the breakup leaked three days after I found them in my office. I finished filming, Jackson flew back home to Idaho, and I tried to pretend that everything was okay. Trace, my agent, manager, assistant, and the rest of the team knew that the storm would come, and we did our best to weather it.

We had tried the joint statement because my agent was killer and forced Dallas to do it. We said we had parted ways amicably and needed space.

Only Dallas wasn't like anyone else.

The paparazzi loved him.

I was just the bitter woman, after all. Not that they knew he had cheated. Because the world didn't need to know, they didn't know that I had been sucker-punched. But I'd been so stupid to think that Dallas could ever love me.

The world didn't need to know the truth because, no matter what, I would be the bad guy. I would either be too old, not good enough, or too good, a whore, or something else.

Dallas could do no wrong, and I was the one the paparazzi chased.

I tried to head to my agent's office, but the paparazzi and others who loved Dallas blocked the way.

Because, of course, I had been the one to break us up. Some believe that he had dumped me, but most assumed I thought I was too good for him. So, I was the one that "broke his heart" as he tried to rally his emotions.

That's the way the media twisted, no matter what my team did.

Dallas and that cruel smile of his were just better at the game.

The next day I tried to get groceries, going as incognito as possible, but cameras and Dallas's fan club blocked me.

So, I sat inside my house, the media camped outside the neighborhood, some even breaking through security to be outside my door.

"Am I going to lose this job?" I asked, my hand shaking with nerves.

My manager sighed on the other end of the line. "No, you're not. They still want you, but they need a little space from this incident. You need a break, just like you planned."

I swallowed hard. "I didn't do anything wrong. He was cheating on me."

"He was. But he's also a man that can do no wrong. You know the way things work. The only way we could win here is if we twisted it so he's the bad guy, but then you're still the shrew who went after him or not good enough." I sputtered, and she continued. "You know I don't believe that. You know I believe in your privacy. And I'm doing all that I can, but maybe you should leave LA for a bit. Go somewhere. Relax. You know what you need to do. Just breathe. You have two hard shoots coming up soon. Use this time to regroup like we planned."

"But then I'm just running with my tail between my legs."

"You're saving your sanity. Let me deal with Dallas out here."

I bit my lip. All I wanted to do was call my best friend to hear her advice, but she was out of the country, in a different time zone, probably on stage right now singing to thousands. We had spoken the day before, and she had threatened to fly out here and save me, but I didn't want to worry her.

I didn't want to worry anyone.

I thought about the last place I had been relaxed, even though I'd held a worry in my gut. I picked up the phone and made the plans.

I would run, I would save myself, and I would figure out what to do.

Because here wasn't working, and once again, I wasn't good enough.

And I had the entire city to remind me.

———

I pulled into Wilder Retreat and Winery, a resort I had been to for a wedding. It had been calm, soothing, and just what I needed.

There were questions that I needed answers to hear as well.

Eli Wilder stood at the entrance, hands in his jeans pockets as he waited for me. I swallowed hard and got out of the black sedan that I'd taken from the airport.

"Bethany, I would say it's good to see you, but from what I can tell, maybe not."

My lips twitched, and I tried to hold back tears. Why was I going to cry with this stranger? It didn't make any sense. I didn't even know the Wilders. This place had been the first that came to mind and I didn't know why.

Then again, maybe I did.

"It's been an eventful couple of weeks." I shrugged as I went to pull out my suitcases from the car. Eli waved me off as the Wilder team and my driver moved my things around.

"We'll get you set up at the cabin. Don't you worry."

I gave him a wobbly smile, glad I still had my dark sunglasses on, and rolled my shoulders back.

I was Bethany Cole. I could act my way out of a paper bag. The world didn't need to see how I felt.

"Thank you for having me on such short notice. I truly appreciate it."

"We've got you, Bethany. Now come on, let's get you relaxed."

I nodded and followed him, knowing I wasn't going to relax, not just yet.

I might be running from things I couldn't change, but there was one thing I could change here.

One person that I was going to confront.

Because I couldn't do anything about Dallas.

I could do something about Everett Wilder.

It was about time I did.

# Chapter Two

## Everett

"We have a full booking for the next month," Eli said as he went over his reports.

I nodded and looked down at my notes. "Which is good. Because we have a few updates to do. East will go over them with you."

"We still in the black?" Eli asked, brow raised.

I nodded. "We're doing good." I knocked on wood. "Though it could always be better."

"So I hear." Eli laughed.

"Anyway. Full bookings are good. Kendall's doing

well in the restaurant. The winery has its new label coming out. Alexis is working her ass off on the weddings, and Elliot is bouncing around from event to event. We've got it handled. We're right at the cusp of something. What? I don't know."

My brother just shook his head. "For somebody who's supposed to have their finger on the pulse of everything, shouldn't you know more?"

"I'm trying," I said with a laugh. "If we're done here, I'm starving, and I'm in the mood for mac and cheese."

"Does that mean Kendall left you some mac and cheese in your fridge that you're going to reheat?" Eli asked.

"I know exactly what I'm in the mood for, thank you very much."

Eli just laughed and we put away our things, then I headed back to my cabin on the other side of the property. I liked living near my brothers, even though some of them were starting to move off into their own homes. But, for the first couple of years, when we were together and were focusing on the property and coming together as Wilders, it was nice. It felt like we finally knew what the hell we were doing—and were getting to know one another again. Considering sometimes I felt like I didn't know myself when I looked in the mirror these days, that was good. It was hard for me to reconcile the fact that some memories from my past were never coming back. That getting my head knocked in the way that I had, sometimes made the numbers on my screen swirl into a whirlpool, but I figured it out. All of my brothers had their own issues from their time in the service.

I wasn't the only one.

I went to work in my kitchen, hitting up the best five-cheese macaroni and cheese there was thanks to my sister-in-law, and went through the rest of my to-do list for the next day.

I needed things to be in order. I had to go through my to-do list daily to make sure I didn't mess things up. I had notes all around the house to make sure that I was ready to go, and my phone was never not at my side. I never used to be like this. I used to remember every-thing, but now, having a checklist for my day was how I focused and how I'd made the best of it.

I was digging into the best macaroni and cheese of my life, even reheated, when my doorbell rang. I frowned and walked over, bowl still in my hand, and nearly dropped the whole thing when I opened it.

*She* stood there.

Bethany.

Her long brown hair framing her face, her bright eyes that called to me.

Every time I saw those on the screen, I felt like I

knew her, felt like she was everything. It was such a weird goddamn crush.

She stared at me as if searching for something and then narrowed her gaze.

"Bethany. Hi. I didn't know you were coming. Are you staying at the resort? Wait, do you need help figuring out where to go? I can get you to a cabin." I set down my macaroni and cheese.

She just shook her head, her eyes widening. "You really don't remember. You have no idea."

I blinked, wondering at the venom in her tone. "Remember? I remember you. Of course, I know who you are."

"Oh, you remember me from our walk, and what, from a movie or two? But, Everett, you don't remember the fact that we fucked?" she snarled, her gaze narrowing.

That dirty word coming out of that sweet mouth nearly rocked me to my core, and I looked at her, shaken.

Because there was no way I could have ever slept with Bethany Cole and not remembered.

Because I *knew* Bethany Cole.

I'd had that silly crush on her for far too long, and if I had ever touched Bethany Cole—other than holding her hand for a second to help lead her down the path when she had almost fallen off a brick walkway—I would have remembered.

"Are you sure you have the right brother?" I blurted, embarrassed. Because there were six of us, she could have slept with another Wilder brother. That made my stomach hurt, and yet I knew it was the wrong thing to say as soon as the hurt crossed her face.

"You're lucky I don't believe in hitting people because I could slap you for that. I know which Wilder I slept with, Everett. I just can't believe you don't remember. I thought you were one of the good ones. And then you walked away and never came back. And now look. You don't remember me, which is *fine*. It would probably be better if most people forgot me."

She whirled on her heels and stomped away. I ran after her, gripping her elbow.

"Bethany. Are you serious?"

"Of course, I'm serious." Her eyes filled before she blinked it away, the steel temptress in place of the crying waif. "You don't know me. *Fine*. I get it. You don't want to remember that night? *Fine*. But don't lie to me. And don't treat me like shit. I am done being treated like shit by everybody who thinks that they own me because I am on their stupid video screens. Fuck you, Wilder."

"I don't remember," I whispered, grasping for any semblance of who I was before everything changed.

*But I couldn't remember.*

"Of course, you don't remember. We weren't drunk but, apparently, you forgot everything about that night like I was nothing."

I shook my head. "No. I don't remember."

"Fine. I'm so happy that you can forget. I'll do the same." Her eyes filled again, but she tried to turn away as if that could stop the memory of her tears searing into my brain.

Anger pounded at my temples. But not at her. Never at her. "You didn't have your head nearly blown off when a bomb exploded near you. So, I'm sorry if I don't remember you. I don't even remember what my mom looks like without a fucking photo these days. I'm sorry. I wish I could goddamn well remember because that is something that I would want to remember. I'm sorry, Bethany. I don't remember. I'm sorry." My head pulsed, and I pressed my fingers to my temples, taking a deep breath, trying to focus.

"Everett? Are you serious?" She moved forward, but I took a step back as a flash of memory assailed me, one after another.

A sweet smile.

A flash of lips.

A laugh that went right to my toes.

And then bile filled my throat, and I staggered to the

side. Bethany was saying something, screaming my name, or maybe she was whispering it. I didn't know. But I fell to my knees, and then her hands were on me, or maybe it was just a dream.

Just like a memory I had forgotten long ago.

And then there was nothing.

---

Voices murmured around me and I tried to ignore them. I just wanted to go to sleep. To let my head rest after what felt like years of headaches and nausea.

All I wanted was to stay asleep.

"He's going to wake up, right?" Elliot asked, his voice low. It was odd because Elliot was always bouncing, moving from place to place, subject to subject. He never had worry in his tone. And yet that was all I heard.

"He's going to be fine. They said he isn't in a coma or anything, just taking his time to wake up."

That was East, my twin.

I knew that voice. The growly one, but rarely spoke up unless he was growling about something or another. My best friend, when he let me.

Out of all of my siblings, he and I were the closest, although it didn't always feel like it these days.

And if he and Elliot were here, I had to wonder where everyone else was. And hell, where I was at this point.

I slowly forced my eyes open, knowing I wasn't going to be going back to bed anytime soon. Not even with the slight headache already pulsating behind my eyes.

"There you are," Elliot said, his grin wide.

I shut my eyes again tightly, the overhead lights bright. East cursed under his breath, and then stood up. It wasn't until the light behind my eyes dimmed slightly that I realize he must've gone to the light switch. I open my eyes again cautiously, taking my time this time.

"What happened?" I croaked. My throat hurt, everything hurt. I reached up and rubbed my throat, grateful that I could feel everything. At least it wasn't as bad as the first time I'd woken up in a hospital like this. Only East had been by my side. And that was only by happenstance. We hadn't been deployed together, but when I had been nearly blown up by that roadside bomb, they'd sent me to the closest hospital. East had been nearby, and since he was one of the famous Wilder brothers, his CO let him stay with me since the others couldn't. It was Elliot who had come by next, a semblance of what we were doing today. That was because of Elliot's job as a medic. None of my other brothers had been able to come to the hospital until later. And even then it was mostly when I was back stateside.

I never blamed them. We all had a job to do, serving Uncle Sam in the ways that we had. Them not being able to be at my beck and call after I had been in the attack just meant that they were able to take staggered shifts later. Just like we had done when Evan had been hurt. Like countless others. Just like we had done when our sister had needed us.

"How are you feeling?" Everett asked as he checked my chart. He wasn't in the medical profession anymore, and probably shouldn't be looking at my chart, but I didn't care. I didn't keep secrets from my siblings anymore, at least I didn't think so. I told them everything I could remember, not that it was much these days. But that was a matter for another time.

"I feel like my head has been stuck in a vise for a while. But I think I'm okay. What happened?" I asked, as I tried to sit up.

My twin pushed me back down, a glare on his face. "Stop moving too quickly. You going to give yourself a headache worse than you already have."

"I'm fine," I lied.

East just scowled.

"We don't really know what happened." Elliot

cleared his throat. "We just heard one of our guests shouting for us, and East came running since he was closest. The rest of us followed suit, and then brought you in to the hospital. The doctors are going to run more tests, but it looks like you passed out from your headache."

I sighed. "I can't believe I passed out from pain. How weak is that?"

Shame crawled over me. Every single one of my brothers dealt with issues in one way or another from their time as an active-duty member of the Air Force. I was no different from them. But here I was, the only one in the hospital who passed out from a headache.

"Don't you dare put yourself down for that," East growled. "You know that you don't have control over that. I'm just glad that you are alive. Damn it."

And with that, my twin stood up, and paced out of the room. Elliot sighed.

"Sorry about that. You know East. He gets growly and walks away from the problem. The doctor should be in soon, especially because you know our dear brother is going to go find them."

I rubbed my temple, annoyed with myself. "The headache is bad. This one snuck up on me, or I would have been better prepared. I guess it just happened quickly."

Images of Bethany hit me again, her smile, her anger. The pain in her face.

"Bethany."

Elliot narrowed his gaze. "So, you remember her. She was the one that found you. She's staying here, well, for reasons of her own that I guess we'll figure out soon. But she was the one that shouted for help. I'm glad that she was there for you, though. Because I don't want to think about what would've happened if it took us until morning to find you alone in your house."

I sat up then, ignored the way that my stomach rolled, and licked my lips.

I remembered her. I remembered as much as I thought I was going to at least. The night in LA. I had been there to visit a friend, and ended up meeting Bethany. I had known who she was before I kissed her, but I hadn't cared. And then we had a brief time together before I shipped out. I had told myself it was all a dream. At least that's what I think happened before the attack.

Because she had been a celebrity, I hadn't been some dumb airman. It was just the two of us for one weekend, and then I was supposed to call her.

"How could I have forgotten her?" I whispered.

Elliot's gaze narrowed. "What do you mean?"

I shook my head and immediately regretted it. "Nothing."

"That's not nothing."

"It's nothing important." Or, at least it wasn't anything I was going to mention. Because I had forgotten Bethany long before this moment. I had forgotten to call her because I had been hurt almost as soon as I had gotten to my destination for my deployment, and things had spiraled from there. I had gone back to work eventually, had been able to be a full and functioning member of the Air Force, but I had lost moments.

I had lost Bethany before I even had her.

She blamed me. No wonder she hated me. No wonder she cursed at me and hated me.

I'd left her high and dry. And if I remember the timing right, she had ended up with Dallas soon after.

I was such a damn idiot.

"You should know that she's here to hide from the paparazzi. Nobody else knows she's on the property other than us."

I froze, looked over at my brother. "What happened? Is she okay?"

Elliot gave me a look that said I was too focused on the girl that they all knew I had a crush on. They didn't know the half of it.

And neither did I, apparently.

"She will be okay. From what I can tell, that douchebag cheated on her, at least that's what I think. The press is being tight lipped, but some are whispering. All they are really saying for sure is that she and Dallas broke up, and now she's run away from LA to hide out. They don't know where she is, and we've got to do our best to keep it that way. But she's here, hurting, and just saved your life. It's been an eventful few hours."

I swallowed hard, a metallic taste coating my tongue.

No wonder Bethany looked so hurt when she had yelled at me. Because I had forgotten her. Had hurt her, even if I hadn't known, hadn't meant to.

But I wasn't the only one hurting her.

The doctors came in then and reminded me to do my meditation and to take my meds, but I couldn't help but think about the woman that was still at the resort.

Hurting, alone, and someone from my past I was just now remembering.

But she was a movie star. A near Oscar-winner.

And I was just Everett Wilder. Broken in more ways than one.

Barely a memory for either one of us.

# Chapter Three

Bethany

I tried not to let it bother me that Everett's brothers had sought me out to tell me that he would be okay. I ignored the deep relief slamming into me when they said he'd be home soon. I couldn't deal with any more emotions than I already had at the moment.

And based on how they told me, I knew that Everett hadn't mentioned why I was at his cabin. Or how I knew him. I didn't let that little hurt get to me because it *didn't* hurt.

He hadn't remembered me for a valid reason and, from the sound of it, he had almost died. My personal feelings of rejection shouldn't matter at all. And they didn't. And though I knew that his brothers had told me since I had witnessed it, I still needed to see him myself.

That didn't make any sense to me, though. It wasn't like I knew Everett. I just knew the memory of him. A memory that I wasn't ready to fully deal with, even though I had gone to his cabin to confront him.

I still wasn't sure why I'd even done that. Maybe because everything else in my life was in turmoil, going in a thousand different directions. Maybe I just wanted one answer.

Or maybe I just wanted to be angry at somebody I could see. Somebody that wasn't the media or Dallas.

I cringed, thinking of Dallas.

I couldn't believe that he had cheated on me.

No, that was wrong. I had seen the way that he had so much chemistry with everybody else around him. That was who he was, the leading man who could lead anywhere.

Dallas was charismatic and gorgeous, and to others, perhaps, he looked selfless. I knew that had never been the case. He had always been a little self-centered, a little too focused on what was good for him. But in LA, that was every actor. I was selfish often because I needed to focus on my own goals, my health, my career, and my body to ensure that I was making the right decisions for my work.

Perhaps it wasn't always the healthiest attitude, but it was what I needed to do to become the person I was. It was inherent in the job—a requirement. Yet Dallas had always taken that one step further. Every job that he did had to be the most important one. They were steppingstones on his path. And while I understood that, hell, I thought we would both do the same thing, he had always been a little more jealous, a little more angry that I was reaching milestones before him.

After all, I won the Golden Globe the year before he did, right when we'd started dating. However, I'd always been grateful that our awards circuit wasn't during the same time. That would've been exhausting for us, even if the media had jumped on the comparisons like the thieves of joy they are quicker than I could've imagined.

I had been able to work with his favorite director before he could. However, the director and team had approached me and not the other way around. I thought that was a boon for myself, but Dallas hadn't liked it.

I had a full five-movie contract with the large superhero franchise that had been Dallas's dream. He was only just now getting cast as a side character with promise of a future, but not yet set in stone.

I had been so proud of him at the time, ignoring the

snide looks and remarks that the only reason he had gotten it was that he was sleeping with me. I hadn't thought that was true, but then again, I didn't know. I didn't know what the directors, producers, and staff were looking for when they cast Dallas.

Was it the press that had said Hollywood's dream couple had trouble at home?

Because that sure wasn't the case now.

I looked at my phone, and scowled at the headlines.

"Bethany dumped."

"A-list star goes into seclusion after being found wanting."

"Oscar hopeful found alone, with no one on her arm for this awards season."

"Click here to see the new romance between Hollywood's new 'It Couple.' Bethany is nowhere to be found."

I scowled at the headlines, annoyed with myself for even caring.

I didn't even know why I had opened up the home page. It wasn't like I even had to search my name. No, we were front-page news. There were wars, famine, political exiles, and constant pain all around the world. But we were the second news story, right under a massive earthquake that killed hundreds of people on the other side of the world.

I pressed my lips together and quickly texted my manager, ensuring we were donating to the relief fund for that one. She responded quickly, saying we had since I had already asked her. My brain wasn't all there yet, and I was repeating things when I usually didn't.

While she had my attention, we went over a few more charities that I wanted to donate to, and I knew that soon I needed to donate my time, but not when I would be more of a hindrance than a help. That was what happened when the media wanted to get a picture of my face and pain and upset over losing Dallas.

So, I would wait until the crush died down a bit before I could go in person to help where I could. Maybe I would do it outside of the states, in a place where nobody knew me, and I would just be a pair of strong hands.

I should've done that instead of coming here, but I was just so tired.

My phone buzzed. I thought it was my manager again, but it was Tonya, letting me know that she was taking care of my LA house before going on her vacation.

I smiled softly, knowing Tonya needed time as well. We both worked long hours, and we were a good team, but I knew she needed some time away from the job that was Bethany Cole.

Another text.

**Trace:** *I let you go off by yourself because I checked the Wilders out. We did recon. You're safe. But if you need me, I'm there. I don't like you being on your own.*

I smiled at that, even though I was feeling hemmed in.

**Me:** *I need space. I need alone time. I'm okay here.*

**Trace:** *I'll be there in two days to check it out regardless.*

I rolled my eyes, knowing that he was doing his job. I just hated that he needed to do it.

My phone buzzed one more time and I nearly threw it across the room, wanting to check with the Wilders again just to see if Everett was okay, and because I had that thought, I looked down at the readout.

Dallas Huntington.

That was how he was in my phone. Not some pet name that I had never called him, not even just his first name.

He was always "Dallas Huntington." *The* Dallas Huntington.

That was how he had put himself on the phone, and I had let it go, laughing because he liked being on a two-name basis with me.

I didn't know why he was calling. I knew it wasn't to say he was sorry or to get me back. That's not what he wanted. No, he wanted to cash in on the attention. Because the man in the situation, even if he was the one with his dick in somebody else, would always come out on top.

I was the Sad Lady who had nobody and would die alone.

It didn't matter that I loved cats and thought a woman living alone with cats was a wonderful thing because that meant she was taking care of fur babies that needed her. All that mattered was that Hollywood was a cruel place sometimes. Or perhaps it was always a cruel place, and I was just tired.

I hit ignore, wondering what Dallas wanted from me.

He already had a new girlfriend, his name in the headlines, and two new jobs that would catapult him into the stardom he thought he deserved.

He didn't need me anymore. So I didn't need to listen to him.

I was about to turn off my phone, knowing that nothing good would come out of it, when my agent's name flashed on the screen. I rubbed the back of my neck; I could feel a migraine coming on. I picked it up, letting my breath out slowly.

"Bethany," she said, her voice low, gritty. Maxine Marshall had brought me out of obscurity—in her words

—and I didn't usually argue. She was harsh, to the point, and yet caring at the same time.

I didn't know how she made it work, but in the end, it didn't matter. Because she did.

"Maxine," I said after a moment.

"I would ask how you're doing, but we already know it's not great."

I let out a laugh. She didn't even know the half of it. She had no idea about Everett, and she wouldn't, because that wasn't going to go beyond my thoughts. She didn't need to know that I had watched a man collapse in front of me. If the press had heard about it, it would be one more thing for them to burn me for.

"Well, I'm here. At the Wilders'."

"Good. They're good people, and will keep you safe."

Alarm shot up my spine. "Did you get another letter?" I asked. I had gotten a few hate letters over my time in this business, and they had started to increase when Dallas and I became serious. That happened when you dated a hot celebrity with his own fandom.

"No, we haven't. I'll let you know as soon as we do. You told us not to hide them from you, and we won't. Even if I don't agree."

"Maxine."

"No, I'm sorry. I didn't mean to bring that up. I

meant stay safe from the paparazzi. The Wilders have security on their property, and while people might spot you there, it's still spaced out enough that you should be fine. Nobody's going to go outside of San Antonio, Texas, to find you."

"I'm going to knock on wood," I said after a moment.

"Good idea." I heard an echo of a knock against her desk, and my lips twitched.

"How much time do you want me to take off?" I asked, my voice soft.

"We scheduled this time off for you. I know you wanted to try to work and work and work, but I, as your agent, am telling you it's okay to breathe. Do it. You have more than enough coming soon. You're allowed to take this moment for yourself."

"I want them to forget about me. At least about everything that they're saying in the press. I can't let them forget about me completely if I want to keep my jobs."

"And that's *my* job. Your job is to relax, maybe find a cowboy in secret. Or cowgirl. Anything you can do just to not think about that Dallas."

That made me laugh. "No cowboys for me. Although, now that I think about it, coming to Texas to try not to think about Dallas probably wasn't the best idea."

"It's not like the winery area is in Dallas. You're fine. It was just a coincidence." Maxine sighed. "Be safe. This will all blow over soon."

She hung up without a goodbye, and I hoped she was right. Only I had a feeling if Dallas had his way, she wasn't going to be. Dallas liked his name in the headlines.

And if he had to drag me down over and over again to make it happen, he would.

I was about to turn my phone off when it buzzed with a new text. I wanted to scream, and then I smiled.

My best friend's name flashed on the screen, and I laughed after I read what she sent.

**Lark:** *As soon as I get back to the states, we are having Wine Wednesdays.*

**Me:** *Can we make it wine every day?*

**Lark:** *Anything you want, princess. I wish I could be there, but I can't get out of the tour. Not only would it be bad for business, I don't want to hurt my fans like that.*

**Me:** *You do not have to come here. And I don't want to hurt your fans either. They love you, and they deserve this time. They deserve you. And you deserve them.*

**Lark:** *I sure hope so. I'll be back soon, and we will have that wine every day that ends in y. Be safe, and I'll start looking up hexes.*

I threw my head back, laughed again, and said goodbye, missing her more than usual. We were usually in the same area when we worked, but this was her first European tour, a singer-songwriter multi-Grammy-winning artist. She was brilliant, worked harder than anyone I knew, and oddly hated the limelight at the same time.

But that was Lark, a contradiction in beauty and talent.

I finally turned off my phone, knowing if I didn't, it would ring again. If they truly needed to get in touch with me, they would contact one of my team, and they would get a hold of me somehow. They always had a way.

I rubbed the back of my neck and realized that even though I loved this little gray farmhouse cottage, I needed to take a walk. To breathe in that Texas cedar, probably break out into hives with my allergies, but just enjoy myself. No more phone calls, no more worries.

If I happened to come in contact with the Wilders, well, maybe that was okay. I made my way outside and down the path and continued walking towards the main area of the inn.

From what I remembered from the first and only time I stayed here before, the Wilder brothers had all gotten out of the military—though I didn't know which branch—and bought this place together.

It was gorgeous, though I didn't know how it ran. There were two main buildings when you first drove down the long and winding road. They looked almost like an Italian villa. One where the main inn was located, and the other was more of an eatery and checking-in point. There was even a small gift shop and tasting room. But I knew that the main tasting room was attached to the winery, which was just down the road on their property as well.

There were not only individual rooms in the main building, but other cabins were dotted around the property. Some hidden, some a little more out in the open. I was staying in one of them and was grateful that it had been available when I needed it.

Everett lived on the property, as did some of his brothers, but I didn't know if they all did.

Why was I here?

Of all the places I could've gone and the multitudes of places I could've hidden, I came here.

To Everett Wilder.

The man from my past, though I should not be thinking about him at all.

I pushed that from my mind and soaked in the beauty of the twisted oak trees and the bright blue skies. The grounds were a mix of lush greenery, open fields, and old farmland. I knew vines on the very edge of the property produced the wines the Wilders made. I'd seen them from afar when I was here for that wedding. Maybe I would go and take a tour, sample the wine, and have a cheese plate. I had an open-ended reservation here, something I was grateful for, and I knew that the Wilders had done that for me because of my name. At least, that's what I thought. If I could use my publicity for something, maybe I would use it for that because it wasn't helping me with anything else.

I turned the corner and nearly ran smack into two women that I recognized. Alexis Wilder was the wedding planner, with honey-brown hair, blond high-lights, and bright hazel eyes.

I knew the other woman worked for the winery, though I wasn't sure what position. Maddie had her long blond hair wrapped into braids around her head, and her bright blue eyes seemed to sense everything.

I looked over at both of them and waved awkwardly.

"Hi. Sorry for startling you," I said, trying not to be awkward. I spoke in front of people for a living. I was good at it, and yet I couldn't seem to don my actress persona.

Instead, I was just awkward teenager Bethany all over again.

Alexis grinned. "It's good to see you. You settle in

okay? I was going to come and check on you later, even though I know that Naomi would, as well."

Naomi was the innkeeper and had indeed checked on me along with Eli, Alexis's husband.

"I settled in wonderfully. I was just going for a walk and trying to remember some of the histories of the Wilders. I mean, of the business."

The girls shared a look, and I wondered what they were saying without words.

Maddie cleared her throat. "We are happy to show you around. We were taking a walk before lunch so we can bug Kendall for some good food."

"Kendall is not only my sister-in-law, but the chef of the establishment. Come on. We will take you around." She paused. "If you want."

"I would love that," I said honestly, my shoulders relaxing. "Tell me about the Wilders."

"The Wilders are six growly brothers, and one sister that lives up in Colorado," Maddie explained with a laugh.

I grinned. "I meant the property."

"Oh, I figured," Alexis said with a laugh.

"We are the Wilder Retreat and Winery, although we also call ourselves a resort because we have the amenities you need at a resort, other than an ocean. If I could just plop us right down on the beach, then I'd be happy," she added.

"I almost went to a beach, but, I don't know, this place called me," I said, not mentioning Everett.

"That makes me happy to hear," Maddie added. "This place was started by a retired Air Force service member, who sold it to the Wilders. When all of the brothers retired from the Air Force, they bought it up, and each learned a new job." Maddie shook her head. "I'm still not sure exactly how they did that, but I used to work with the old owners, and while I loved them, I do appreciate the direction the Wilders are going with this. They are trying their best, working hard, and making it work."

"They each have their own special skill, and what they don't know, they hired on or learned." Alexis shrugged. "Hence why I'm the wedding planner here."

"So you weren't already married to Eli when you started here?"

Alexis shook her head. "No, though we had met before, it's a long story."

"I'd like to hear it sometime," I said honestly. I wasn't good at making friends. I tried, but it was hard in my line of work.

But with the way that Alexis smiled softly, I thought

I had said the right thing. "I think over a glass of wine that Maddie provides, that would be an awesome story."

"Well, since I am the tasting room and wine club manager, it is my job. The place functions as its own little society here, and we do our best to make it thrive. We host weddings, other events, honeymoons, anniversaries, and retreats. We try to provide everything that you need, including a shoulder if you need it." She cringed. "I'm sorry. That was probably a little too forward."

I shook my head, laughing. "It's fine. I assume all of you know what happened."

Alexis frowned. "No, we know what the media says happened, but we don't know what actually happened. We follow enough celebrity gossip to realize that not all of it is true. So, if you'd like to talk about it over that glass of wine, or some of Kendall's amazing food, we're here. If you don't want to talk about it at all, we can continue walking and see more of the area. Anything that you want."

For some reason, I wanted to cry, to hold these two women that were near strangers close to me. They seem to understand it more than nearly anyone else in my life. Lark got me. Even my team somewhat got me, but not most other people. I felt most days that I was an island in an endless ocean that didn't quite understand that it wasn't supposed to erode the sand from the shore.

"Maybe one day. Although wine and yummy food do sound good," I said.

"That sounds like a plan." Maddie looked up and smiled. "Now I guess you can meet with a Wilder as well. He knows more about this place than anyone. Although, you might have already met him," she added with a frown.

"Since you saved him, I would assume so," Alexis said softly, curiosity in her gaze.

I turned, knowing they probably had more questions I could never answer, and saw *him* walking up the path.

Relief hammered into me and my knees nearly buckled. He looked whole, healthy. Not like he had been passed out in my arms the night before.

I didn't know why he was here, walking alone, when he should be in bed.

But I was grateful for it.

Then he met my gaze, and I remembered all over again.

Remembered who he had been.

And remembered the night that had changed everything.

# Chapter Four

Everett

B*efore*

"How is LA so hot?" I asked as I wiped the back of my head, grateful for my newly shorn buzz cut.

Clayton rolled his eyes. "You're a wimp. Virginia is humid as hell. How the hell did you get so used to fall weather so quickly?" the other man asked as he meandered down Hollywood Boulevard.

I took in the sights, stared at the stars with celebrity names on them, and wondered why we were here. We only had so much leave and were being deployed in the next month. Instead of going anywhere else and relaxing, Clayton had wanted to come out to LA to talk to an ex-girlfriend. Thanks to his parents, he had a spare ticket and hotel room, so I came along.

All of my brothers were overseas a few months themselves, so it wasn't like I could visit them, and my younger sister was out of the country as well. So instead of staying at home without my large family and pretending I wasn't nervous about the upcoming deployment, I was in LA.

"I am particular about the heat on my skin. And yes, I realize we're about to be headed out to a desert and I should get over it. I just can't help it. It's hot."

"But we have palm trees now. We are not going to have palm trees wherever the hell we're going later," he grumbled.

I reached out and squeezed his shoulder. He looked over at me and grinned. "See? You do like me."

I rolled my eyes as Jericho, Jennifer, and Todd turned the corner and waved at us.

"What's next? We need to go down to the pier. Or the beach. Is the pier on the beach?" Jericho asked as he rubbed his temple.

Jennifer rolled her eyes. "Think about what you just said."

"I heard it as I was saying it. It doesn't make me any less dumb." Jericho blushed. "Still love me?" he asked, fluttering his eyelashes.

Jennifer shoved at his shoulder playfully and they all laughed before we continued our trip down the famous street, taking photos and even getting a kind tourist to take a group photo of us.

This wasn't the trip we were counting on, not when we thought maybe we could head to one of my brothers' places, but at the last minute, Eli had been forced out on a deployment. He had offered up his house for us to chill at since he was near a lake to relax. We had almost done it, and then Clayton's free trip came up, so here we were.

Clayton's parents wanted him to meet up with his ex-girlfriend to see if they could work it out. Their families both came from money, had similar connections, and long ties.

I didn't know what Clayton would do about it or if he even really liked this girl, but it was a free trip across the country, and the five of us were together.

We had two more women as part of our group, but they were with their husbands on their own trips before we all got deployed.

Jennifer and I had dated briefly. We had been young —eighteen, in fact—and realized that even casually dating somebody that would be by your side day in and day out in war probably wasn't the best idea.

We ended our relationship almost as soon as it began, grateful we were still friends, but I knew that some people still gave Jennifer shit about it.

Because you couldn't be a woman in any profession and have a personal life. At least, that was what my sister and Jennifer had taught me over the past few years.

We ended up hanging out on the beach, Todd and Jericho practically throwing themselves into the calm waves. Clayton was on the phone, presumably with his ex-girlfriend, while Jennifer sat next to me on a beach towel. Shaking her head, she stared up into the blue sky.

"This is nice. Weird, but nice."

I looked over at her. "What's nice? What's weird?"

"It's weird that we're taking this trip so that way we can pimp out our friend for his family. But nice because the weather is good, even if you're growling that you're hot."

"I guess it is weird. I didn't want to think about it as a 'pimping out' situation, but here we are."

"As long as he claims he's happy? That's fine with

me. I don't plan on dating anybody until I'm ready to get out, after my twenty. Too much work."

I narrowed my gaze at her. "Thanks."

"You don't count. A couple of bangs does not make a relationship."

I threw my head back and laughed. "Here I was, just thinking that we were making it work after our relationship. I guess we didn't have one."

She lowered her aviators down her nose. "You know we didn't. But that's okay."

"Thanks for that. Now we better head out to find that taco place where Clayton wanted to meet his girl. Mostly because I'm starving."

At that, Jennifer's stomach rumbled and we laughed before we pulled the guys out of their knee-deep wading in the water and waved over at Clayton.

"You ready to go?" I asked

Clayton nodded. "Yeah. We are meeting at the taco joint. I don't know. I don't think she's really into this either."

"Then why are you here?" I asked softly as we all scrambled into the rental SUV.

"Because my parents asked. Because they're just as scared as any parent would be with their kid in the military. And because I do like Chasity. I'm just not ready to get married and settle down. You know?"

"I know," I whispered.

I let the subject drop, and we went back to making fun of Todd's new flip-flops, which were ridiculous and made of some foam that didn't like the saltwater, before Jericho pulled into the taco joint. It was a hole in the wall but seemed to have decent business, considering there was a line out the door.

"Chasity got us reservations. And yes, this place takes reservations," he said offhandedly.

We followed him, wondering why he needed all of us for this date. Or whatever this was.

I shook my head, then saw a girl with wavy bleached blond hair, brown doe eyes, and a soft smile wave over at Clayton. Clayton smiled wide, his eyes going to warm chocolate as he looked at her, and I met Jericho's gaze. Well, there seemed to be a lot more to Clayton and Chasity than we knew.

We took our table, and each ordered enough tacos and various other California Tex-Mex food to feed an army. Or rather, our squadron.

Clayton introduced Chasity to us, and we all laughed, ate together, and enjoyed the afternoon. She seemed nice, nothing like I imagined she would be considering how he had described her parents. But then again, that was me just being judgy.

Afterward, we went to a bar nearby, to meet up with

some of Chasity's friends. And that's how I ended up dancing to odd techno music, drinking my one and only vodka tonic for the night, and watching my friends slowly get shitfaced as they danced with strangers, having a little too much fun.

Jennifer was just as sober as I was, paying attention to the guys. She came over to me, dancing beside me, both of us keeping our distance.

"Getting them into the SUV and out of somebody else's beds later is going to be difficult," she mumbled.

"You're not their babysitter. As long as they're back at the hotel by 0900 tomorrow, it's fine. We all said we would go our separate ways for the evening if we wanted to. As long as they're safe."

Jennifer rolled her eyes and let out a breath. "Then I'm going to head back to the hotel now. I'm tired."

Alarmed, I stared at her face. "Everything okay?"

"Everything's fine. I just have a headache from the sun. Apparently you were right. It was hot. I'm going to take a taxi."

"I'll walk you out," I said, leaving my drink on the edge of the bar. "I'm done drinking tonight anyway."

"Are you going back to the hotel with me? I trust those guys with my life, but not with gossip."

I heard the warning in her tone, and I nodded. "I'll come right back in so they see that you left alone.

Even if I don't like the thought of you walking out alone."

Todd came up to us, a little weary, and cleared his throat. "I'm tired too. Three drinks were a little too much for me. I'll go home with Jennifer." He cleared his throat again. "In my separate room. Because I know better."

Jennifer laughed and pointed towards the taxi waiting for them. "Okay, knight in shining armor. That works."

I glared between the two of them. "Wait, you going home with Todd instead of me isn't going to cause an issue?"

Todd met my gaze and raised a single brow. And that's when I got it.

Right, none of the guys or I would think that Jennifer and Todd going back to their separate hotel rooms together would be an issue. Because Jennifer and Todd had the same taste in men. I laughed, then waved them off, making them promise to text me once they got back to the hotel.

"Whatever you say, daddy," Todd shouted out of the open window, and I laughed before I turned and slammed into a woman behind me.

I cursed and gripped her shoulders. "Are you okay? So sorry. What an idiot. I should've been watching where I was going." I looked down at her, noticed her soft brown hair and kind eyes, and nearly swallowed my tongue.

Bethany Cole.

I knew this woman. We were in LA. Even if we weren't in Beverly Hills, there were celebrities everywhere. I had even seen three popular action stars walking down the street earlier. Or, possibly impersonators with really good makeup.

This, though, wasn't an impersonator. I'd studied Bethany Cole's face long enough when I watched her movies to know who this was.

I needed to stop staring, or she would call the police on me. And I would not blame her.

"It's okay. I'm fine. Thank you, though." She looked at my hands still on her shoulders, and I quickly dropped them and stuck them in my pockets.

"Sorry about that. Well, walk safely. And you probably will because I won't be around to bump into you."

She shook her head and laughed, before her friend, a woman with long honey-blond hair, pointed towards the bar I had just walked out of.

"Here it is, B. Johnny is playing there tonight."

"Sounds good. Nice to meet you." She smiled at me before she turned.

I cleared my throat. "By the way, I'm going in there,

but I'm not following you. I don't want it to feel weird even though I've just made it weird."

The two women looked at me and laughed, shaking their heads. "No problem. Thank you for warning me that you're going to be the weird stalker behind me." She winked as she said it, but I still felt like an idiot. I was getting good at that.

I did indeed follow her inside and went back to my corner of the bar. I sat laughing with my friends as Bethany and the other woman went to talk with the band.

Of course, she would know the band. She was Bethany freaking Cole.

Nobody else seemed to really realize who she was, maybe that was because most people in here were slightly drunk and the lighting wasn't great. Or maybe I just had a problem.

I wasn't in the mood for another drink, but I was thirsty, so I went up to the bar to get something, waving off the guys as they laughed with a group of girls, and I knew that I wouldn't be seeing them anytime soon. No, they had their game on, and this was what they wanted. Clayton was cuddling into Chasity, and Jericho was with one of her friends. More power to them.

I walked up to the bar, ordered a soft drink, and then

leaned my back against the bar as I waited. That's when I caught sight of them.

A man crowded over Bethany, a little drunk and a little too handsy with her. I saw the way that she stiffened and tried to back out of his touch, but he wasn't having it.

He put his hand on her arm. When she flinched, I knew that was it. I wasn't in the mood to end up in jail tonight, but nobody laid a hand on a woman in that manner without her permission.

I walked up to the man, and I was grateful that I seemed to have an inch and at least twenty pounds of muscle on him. I tapped the back of his shoulder and cleared my throat.

"Hey, do we have a problem here?" I asked.

The music was booming, so nobody else really heard us, but I saw Bethany's eyes widen and the guy glare over his shoulder at me.

"I'm just talking to this nice lady over here. We don't need anything from you, asshole."

"See, this is where we're going to have a problem. That's my girl you're holding right there and I don't appreciate it."

The man glared at me. "Seriously? She's yours?"

"I am," Bethany popped up, and I was grateful. It probably wasn't the best way to handle the situation, but I wasn't sure what else I could do other than start a fight. Maybe if he thought that she was taken, he would back down.

Because of the man's surprise, Bethany was able to duck out from under his arm and come around to me and put her hands around my waist.

"I told you I was taken. But thank you for keeping me safe in this hallway while I waited for my boyfriend."

The guy glared at me, then at her, before shrugging, taking a sip of his beer, and swaggering away.

"I'm going to be honest. I did not think that would work," I said suddenly, blinking.

Bethany looked up at me. "Oh, same. I thought I would have to kick him in the nuts, or you would. I didn't know if I was ready to watch an actual bar fight. I don't think I've ever seen a bar fight in person."

I chuckled roughly, my adrenaline starting to come down. That's when I realized I was talking to Bethany Cole in a dark hallway. What a weird night.

"I've seen a couple, but I've never been in one. You okay?" I asked, sobering.

She nodded. "I am. My friend had to go home because of an emergency, and I was going to follow her, but I got distracted by a work call. Thank you again." She paused. "Can I buy you a drink?"

I really wished she could. "I was just having a soda, not in the mood to get drunk, you know?"

"Honestly, same. I don't like drinking in public places like this. It always trips me out. Just weird. By the way, I'm Bethany."

"I know." I sputtered. "I'm sorry. I mean, well. Hi, I'm Everett."

Bethany grinned. "So, you did recognize me. I find that so weird. Not that you did, but that anybody does. I'm still not used to this whole thing. Even if I have been doing it for a while now."

"I guess it could be weird. I didn't want you to think that I knew who you were, so I tried to play it cool. So, I just, you know, nearly knocked you down on the sidewalk and now claimed you as my girlfriend. So, all in all, pretty casual."

She shook her head, laughed, and gestured towards the bar. "Well, I can buy you a soda, or there is a donut place a block down. A little quieter, and I just realized I offered to take you to a secondary location. Either I'm a serial killer, or you are, and you are tricking me into doing your dirty work for you."

I grinned. "Why don't you tell your friend my name and take a photo of me so that way she knows what to tell the authorities. What do you say?"

Bethany smiled and nodded. "That sounds like a plan."

Three donuts later, we were exchanging phone numbers.

Three dates and two days later, my lips were on Bethany's, in my hotel room, not even realizing how we had gotten here.

I hadn't meant to kiss her, hadn't meant to do all of this.

It just happened. Chemistry just happened sometimes.

"This is insane," she whispered. "It's not supposed to happen like this."

Damn straight. "I'm leaving tomorrow. I can't stop kissing you."

"It's okay. We'll figure it out."

And then there was nothing else to figure out. Just my lips on hers.

I slowly moved us towards the bed, which didn't take long considering the hotel room was tiny. Bethany had probably seen bigger hotel rooms in every country she had ever visited, but it didn't matter. Because she wasn't Bethany Cole right now. She was just Bethany.

My Bethany.

In this insane whirlwind of a romance that didn't make any sense.

I continued to kiss her, continued to breathe her in.

When she tugged on my shirt, I let her pull it off quickly, and I did the same to hers, both of us in the moment, barely comprehending.

Her breasts overfilled my hand. I tugged on the cup of her bra and saw her nipples were rosy-pink, luscious, and tight. I licked the bud, sucking and biting down. When she shivered at my touch, I did the same to her other breast.

My cock pressed against the seam of my shorts and I adjusted myself, groaning at the sensation. And then her hand was down my pants, gripping me, and I nearly came right then.

I could barely breathe, could barely do anything, we were stripping off each other's clothes, and we were naked, my nose between her legs, trying to understand exactly how this had happened.

I hadn't been looking for her, hadn't been looking for this. This was all that mattered. It was all that could matter.

And when I sheathed myself in a condom and slowly trailed the tip against her entrance, we both shivered.

"Are you sure?" I whispered,

"Please. Everett. Please. I promise."

And so, keeping her gaze on mine, I tangled my fingers with hers with one hand above her head and then put my other hand on her hip before I slowly, oh so slowly, filled her.

We both groaned at the sensation, shaking, and then we were moving, breathing as one.

I didn't know how it happened, how I was here, but I wasn't going to take it for granted. When we both came, it was an explosion of sensations that made my mind whirl. I held her, holding back tears of my own as I kissed away hers. It didn't seem true that this was happening. But it was, there was no going back. Because I was falling for her, even though I shouldn't. Because she was a celebrity, an actress with the whole world in front of her. And I was leaving to a place where I wouldn't see her for months. Or I could die if I made the wrong move.

But I pushed those thoughts out of my mind and held her close.

And I knew I would call her the next day, and the next, and the next.

And we would make this work. Because this was important. I knew it.

Only I didn't know I would break my phone the next day.

That I would be forced to make decisions I wasn't ready for.

That I would lose everything only a week later.

That I would lose myself in the process.

# Chapter Five

Bethany

As soon as I saw him down the path, Everett was called away by one of the staff members. He walked off along the marble and stone square tiles in the beautiful wedding venue area. I knew that he wasn't ignoring me. That he had a job to do, even if I felt as if perhaps he was working too hard after everything that had happened. Only, I wasn't allowed to think like that. I couldn't govern his life or tell him he was working too hard. That wasn't my job. I barely knew him. We'd only had a few short days together, a single night of passion and heat.

And then he had gone away, never contacting me again. Leaving me alone in my feels and heartache.

Two weeks later, Dallas asked me out and I said yes, both of our managers and agents excited about the potential pairing and the publicity.

I had gone in thinking that this could be a relationship, but Dallas apparently had gone in wondering what this could do for him.

I did not blame Everett for my own choices, although part of me had at first, when things had gotten bad, right before I found out Dallas had cheated on me. And it was all because I'd seen Everett at that wedding. I had seen him in the garden parking area in between the inn and the winery. He'd shown me around, but he hadn't even acknowledged my presence other than treating me kindly as a guest, with a slight bumbling of a man noticing a woman who happened to be in movies.

I needed to get out of my head. I had things to do today that didn't revolve around Everett.

I looked around the small gray cabin that had been decorated to feel homey, classy, and spacious even in the small space. Yesterday, Alexis had told me it was where she had first lived when she came to work for the Wilders.

Now she and Eli lived in a larger home about ten minutes from the Wilder property. Evan, another

Wilder, and his wife, Kendall, their head chef, were also in the process of building a home around fifteen minutes away. Kendall was also nearing her due date with twins.

I had no idea how she could work in the kitchen while being that pregnant, but Alexis and Maddie both promised me that Kendall had a team to help her out.

And from what I knew of the Wilders, even with just casual meetings, I knew that they wouldn't want her to stand on her feet for too long. They seemed to be overly protective and growly that way.

And I didn't know why that appealed to me so much.

Maybe because I never had that. Dallas had been possessive, not protective. That was something that had taken me too long to realize. The difference wasn't something to be taken for granted, even though I had.

I needed to review a few scripts, check my email, read a book, work out, or relax. Do something that wasn't wake up at 4:30 in the morning to either train, workout, rehearse, or be on set. Sometimes I did all of those simultaneously, and I still wasn't sure how I did it, even though I loved it.

Deciding to take my morning coffee out on the porch to look at nature or whatever normal people did, I grabbed my phone so I could look through my email. My team went through most of it for me, with my personal email kept secure and tightly scrutinized.

My phone buzzed as I sat down on the rocking chair, and I smiled.

**Lark:** *Meet any cowboys yet?*

**Me:** *You're the one with that duet with the country music star. You meet more cowboys than I do. Plus, I'm in South Texas, are there cowboys here?*

**Lark:** *That's just something we're going to have to figure out together. It's going to take research. Diligence.*

**Me:** *I don't think I'm in the mood to meet a cowboy. Or any man.*

**Lark**: *I'm sorry. I was just joking with you. Are you okay?*

**Me:** *Honestly, I am far more okay with the breakup than I should be, considering how long we were together. I'm a little more stressed about the betrayal and the paparazzi than anything.*

**Lark:** *At least your heart doesn't hurt. Your pride maybe, that I understand more than anybody. But heartbreak is only good for songs, and even then, I would rather make it up.*

I smiled at that, and we continued to talk about her day, what cities she had left on her European tour, and then we said our goodbyes. I finally went to my email, my coffee almost gone.

I had my usual inbox of some spam, but mostly work things that my agent wanted me to look at when I had time. If they were truly time sensitive, she would have texted or called me.

Then I got to an email that had bypassed my spam filters, and I frowned.

The subject line felt a little ominous. I wondered if it was truly spam. I don't know why I opened it, but I did. I regretted it as soon as I did.

### Subject: the path to say goodbye

*Bethany,*

*You were our sunshine.*

*Our only sunshine.*

*But now the darkness is gray, and you broke our hearts.*

*How could you hurt him?*

*How could you leave us?*

*The world will know what you have done. The world will cry with us.*

*You broke our hearts.*

*You broke us.*

*And you will find your cloudy someday.*

. . .

I blinked as I finished the odd poem that seemed to be a cannibalistic version of the song and shook my head.

I had gotten odd stalker letters before—my agent had a whole folder of them—but this one felt weird.

Our?

Me, Dallas, and who else?

I shook my head, a little worried. Because I didn't know who this was from, I forwarded it to my agent and immediately called her.

"Damn it. Okay, we need to beef up your security. I'll contact the Wilders and the authorities and add it to the folder."

The fact that I had a folder of odd notes like this worried me, but other people in the business constantly told me that this was just the way it was. I didn't want it to be that way. I wanted to act, to find fun and emotion and drama in a character, and breathe life into them on screen.

I didn't want the fans screaming my name and obscenities at me, finding ways into my house, and stalking me around the world.

But one didn't happen without the other. Apparently.

"Let me talk with Eli. He'll be able to help."

"Eli Wilder? The owner?"

"I think all of the brothers own equally," I corrected her, wondering why I did. "Yes, I'll talk with Eli myself. You do the other things, talk to Trace because he'll want to jump on a plane right now, and you can ease him more than I can, but I'll talk with him, too. If my being here is going to hurt the company, I'll go somewhere else where it's easier to keep me safe. I just hate the fact that I have to worry about that. But I'll talk to Eli."

My agent agreed and hung up, and I let out a breath.

"What are you going to talk about with Eli?" Everett asked from the ground by the porch.

I nearly dropped my phone with a yelp and swallowed hard.

"What? How long were you there? What did you hear?" I asked. Considering someone might've just threatened me with an email, I was being a little lax of my own security since I hadn't even been aware of my surroundings. No more. I had to be better about that.

"If you're so worried about that, now *I'm* worried. Talk to me, Bethany. Is something wrong?" He moved up the steps and stood in front of me, tall, broad, and all muscle. He was slightly more slender than he had been when I'd first met him, but he was still in shape and beautiful.

I should stop thinking about those words in relation to him, considering everything that just happened.

"I need to talk to your brother about my security." There was no reason for me to keep it secret, especially if I had to leave. I needed to take care of my own security, and that meant keeping the Wilders aware of what could happen. If I had to leave, I would, but lying and hiding from Everett because I was afraid of feelings or anything else like that wasn't going to help anyone.

Everett's eyes narrowed, and he gave a tight nod. "Talk to me about it. Tell me what happened as we walk to my brother's office. He's there today, working on paperwork."

I frowned as I stood up. "I don't need you to take over everything for me. I can handle this, Everett."

"Of course, you can handle it. You can handle anything. While you do that, you're going to tell me what happened so I can help. We Wilders take care of our staff and our guests. It's what we do."

I ignored the little twinge at the word "guests." Because that's all I was to him. It's all I should be to him. I didn't need to be coddled, but I did need to take my own action.

I sighed and walked into my cabin, putting my coffee cup in the sink and sliding on my shoes. I was wearing soft linen pants and a flowing top and figured I looked fine. I slid large sunglasses on my nose, hoping that would keep me slightly anonymous. I wasn't going to be hiding who I was here completely, I could never do that. But I could at least not stand out like a sore thumb. Everett gave me a once over and nodded before leading me out of my cabin.

I wondered why I felt grateful that he apparently okayed what I was wearing. There was seriously something wrong with me.

"Talk to me."

I sighed. "I got another anonymous email that seems a little threatening. I don't know exactly what it means, my agent is dealing with the authorities. They might call here, too. I just need to let Eli and the rest of you know that I could have a stalker."

Everett cursed a blue streak and I shook my head. "What the hell? Why don't you have any security here? Why aren't you walking around with a big dude with muscles upon muscles the size of Jason Momoa taking care of you?"

That made me laugh. "Jason has bodyguards, too, thank you very much. And I only have them for certain events, especially when the crowd is going to be a bit much. I didn't think I would need them out here. I came out here for rest, relaxation, and, honestly to get away from the paparazzi in LA. I didn't think I needed to hide from someone who was sending notes that are probably just nothing. I get hundreds of letters a week that are just nothing, or talking about my boots, how they hate my work, how they love my work. I'm used to it. It's why I don't want my own social media."

Everett shook his head as we walked down the path towards the main house. "I don't know how you do that. How you handle it all."

I shrugged as if it didn't matter, even though it did. "You get used to it. You have to. I love what I do, even if I don't like everything that comes with it. I honestly don't think that note means much, other than the fact that they don't like that Dallas and I broke up. That's not going to change, but I do need to keep people informed when I get them. Keeping secrets like that only gets people hurt. I learned that a while ago in this business."

Everett gave me a quelling look. "What do you mean?"

"I have friends who had stalkers who got worse. Who find exactly where they live, and get in their homes. It's why I moved into a big house that I don't need behind security that seems a little outlandish. It keeps me as safe as I can possibly be without living out in the boonies. And even then, you can never be too safe. You just get used to it. I don't want to put a burden on any of the Wilders or any of your guests. So, if I have to leave, I will. I promise. I won't bring any problems here."

Everett cursed under his breath again as we walked upstairs towards Eli's office. "You won't be a burden. Or problem. You sure as hell aren't going to go out there alone where somebody could hurt you."

I raised a brow at his tone, and as we walked into Eli's office, his brother did the same thing.

"Okay, why don't you get me up to speed? I just got a call from your agent," Eli said, and I sighed.

"I told her I would handle it."

"I'm sure you can. Want to tell me what happened, and we'll see what we can do?"

I did, and even showed them the email. Everett began to pace as Eli scowled.

"We can handle this. We have security already after a few things happened before." He growled as he said the words, and I looked between the brothers, knowing I was missing something.

"Is everyone okay?" I asked, my voice soft.

Eli nodded tightly. "They are now. We take the security of our family, our team, and our guests seriously. So I'll talk with the security here, make them aware of this note and anything else you get. If you feel the need to add more of your own personal team to the resort, please let us know so that way we can let them know. We're not going to shoo them away because we think we can handle it better. But we'll take care of you."

I looked between them, an odd emotion slamming into me as tears threatened.

"Are you serious?"

Everett let out a laugh that was void of humor. "Of course, we are. You need help."

I blinked. "Most people don't think so," I whispered.

Everett shrugged. "We're Wilders. We're not most people."

For some reason, that made me feel more alone than ever. They had each other and banded together when they needed to. I had my team. I had Lark. But I didn't have anyone else.

How had I let that happen? How had I drifted away from so many friends that I thought I had made over the years to hide behind my work?

Maybe I was just thinking too hard.

We did indeed go over plans with the Wilder security branch and other notes and, in the end, I was exhausted but exhilarated.

I wasn't going to be a burden. This wasn't going to be difficult. We were going to make this work.

If I kept telling myself that over and over again, it would all make sense.

When we were done, my stomach growled and Everett smiled.

"Come on, I'm taking you to get some food."

"You have work to do," I said, immediately shaking my head. "I can handle it on my own."

"We just went over this. You don't have to do it on your own. You need a break, and so do I. Especially after that."

"How's your head?" I asked, studying his face.

He went blank for a minute, and I was afraid I'd said too much and was far too curious.

In the end, he sighed. "I'm fine."

"If you say so. You scared me," I whispered. I hadn't meant to say that out loud, to be so honest. But apparently, today was the day for being honest.

His face closed up for an instant, and then he nodded tightly. "Let's go get something to eat, and I guess I'll tell you. I suppose we have a few things to talk about. After all, you've been so open just now, I guess I should do the same."

He led me down the stairs towards the kitchens, and nerves wrecked me.

Because I was afraid I didn't want to know exactly what he wanted to talk to me about.

Yet, I knew I needed to.

Only, I didn't know why.

# Chapter Six

## Everett

My nerves were buzzing, but this had to be done. Bethany was going through so much of her own worries, things that sent anger through my veins, so me telling her exactly how I had been hurt shouldn't be the end of the world.

At least, that was what I told myself.

I couldn't believe people were threatening her. And it seemed she was so used to it that she had a routine for when someone sent her a nasty email, or letter, or God knew what else. It was just something that she dealt with and moved on.

As if this was just part of life and completely normal.

There might not be much I could do for her, but I would be damned if anybody hurt her on Wilder land.

I opened the service door, allowing Bethany to go in first. "Come on. We'll go bother my sister-in-law for food."

Bethany's lips twitched, even though I knew she was stressed. "I can usually get my own food, considering I am a guest here."

"Oh, sure," I said with a laugh. "But I am truly annoying her. She thinks I'm a pest, and I relish in it."

"You are a pest," Kendall said as she stood over a boiling pot of water, the steam making her face flushed. Or perhaps that was the protruding belly in front of her that stuck out so far it entered a room before she did.

"But you love me." I moved to her, kissed her forehead, her cheek, and then bent down to kiss her belly. I patted it twice, and she rolled her eyes.

"You're very lucky that I gave you permission to do that, because anyone else would be murdered right now."

"I'm just blessed that way."

Kendall looked over my shoulder and I turned, gesturing towards Bethany. "You remember Bethany, don't you?" I asked.

Kendall's eyes widened and she smiled. "It's good to see you again. I'm glad that we made a good enough impression on you that you decided to come back."

Kendall didn't mention why Bethany was here, and I was grateful. We all knew why, but sometimes it was nice to be able to pretend. Plus, it wasn't any of our business.

"I love it here. Thank you all so much for opening this place and allowing me to come back. Of course, I don't think I've ever actually been in here before. It's so busy."

Indeed, it was. Kendall's staff was working nonstop to get lunch prepared, as well as prep for an event that afternoon. Sandy, Kendall's assistant, or perhaps she was called her sous chef, was working up a storm, as was the rest of Kendall's team.

I noticed that nobody was asking Kendall for help and were all purposely doing any work that she might've done in the past. She was nearing the end of her pregnancy, and nobody wanted to overwork her. But telling Kendall to take time off and put her feet up never ended well. At least for the person doing the suggesting.

"We are a well-oiled machine here, at least sometimes." She turned to me. "Let me guess. You're hungry?"

I smiled wickedly. "Of course. I figured I could steal

something to eat from you. And not just for me. Bethany too. She's starving."

Bethany slapped my arm, laughing. "Don't put this on me. You were hungry, too. I heard your stomach growl."

"That's Everett. Always hungry and coming in here for snacks. As it happens, I have a chicken avocado club sandwich with your name on it, as well as pasta salad, a fruit cup, chocolate cake, and homemade sweet potato chips. How's that sound?"

My mouth watered and Bethany held in a groan.

"Okay, I was hungry before, but now I'm beyond starving," Bethany said with a laugh.

"We've got you. I think I have some cheese right here for you." She winked as she said it before waddling off to Sandy.

"Cheese?" Bethany asked.

Kendall looked over her shoulder. "I like cheese. My sisters-in-law all have a cheese fetish, so they let me into their family because of it."

Bethany's eyes twinkled as Sandy pushed Kendall gently out of the way and came towards us.

"I'll make you lunch. Go make sure that Kendall's watching the pot of boiling water." Sandy winked as she said it, going back to work, and I looked over at my sister-in-law.

She scalded lettuce, tapping her foot. It was then that I realized that her shoes were mismatched, and I pressed my lips together.

"They want me to watch boiling water. Earlier, they wanted me to sit down and count deviled eggs. I know what they're doing. It's like they don't know this is my kitchen."

"It's because you don't know how to take time for yourself," I said after a minute, as I gently guided Kendall to a chair. She scowled at me, but when I began to rub her lower back, she let out a groan and finally sat down.

Bethany was right behind me, reaching for a stool to put Kendall's feet up.

Sandy gave us a thumbs-up as she packed our lunches, and Kendall sighed, leaning into my hands.

"I should hate you for this, but this is amazing. Thank you." She looked down at Bethany and blushed. "I cannot believe Bethany Cole is rubbing my ankles. It's like a dream."

Bethany laughed, her whole face brightening. "If you had grapes, I'd feed them to you as well."

"We've got grapes," Sandy called out and somehow magically appeared with a bowl.

Bethany laughed, stood up, and began to feed them to Kendall after she washed her hands. We were technically in Kendall's office, not in the kitchen, so feeding her grapes like this was still okay.

"How can I sign up for this?" Evan asked as he walked in, his eyes only for his wife. He nodded at Bethany and me, then leaned forward, and kissed his wife soundly on the mouth. "Doing okay, baby?"

"The babies and I are doing just fine. I'm being spoiled here, and I don't really know how it happened."

"Because I'm a maniacal planner, and I have my ways," Sandy put in. She held out two boxes for me. "Here are your lunches. Go enjoy the sun, enjoy the day. Relax. I know you had a long night, Everett. I'm sure Bethany could use some time alone, too." She winked at both of us, then headed out, ordering the kitchen around as if it were her sole purpose in life.

"I don't need you guys to pamper me like this," Kendall muttered, but Evan waved us away.

"Seriously, enjoy the day. I've got my wife here."

"Look at you, being all possessive," Kendall whispered, and I quickly ushered Bethany out, giving the two lovebirds privacy.

"They are adorable," Bethany murmured.

"They really are. I love the fact that this is their second time around, and they're stronger than ever."

Bethany frowned at me. "What do you mean?" she asked.

"Evan and Kendall were married before, got divorced, and found their way back to each other. It's kind of romantic."

"Second-chance romance. I didn't think that really happened."

"I think sometimes you meet somebody, and you click, but it's just not the right time. Mistakes are made. Those you can't take back, then you're given that second chance. If you can find the courage to take it."

We were standing in the garden now, the same garden I had met her. Or where I had thought I had met her over a year ago. It turns out I knew her before, and the memories were back, even if some parts were faded, shaded.

But I was remembering.

And I hated that I had hurt her.

"What happened, Everett?" she whispered.

"Do you remember my friends? Clayton, Jericho, Jennifer, and Todd?" Saying their names sent jagged shards down my throat, twisting in my heart.

"You're...remembering?"

"Yes. When I saw you? It started coming back. Not everything, but I'm trying." I let out a breath. "I'm sorry, Bethany. I'm trying."

She studied my face and nodded. I wished I knew what she was thinking. "I met your friends for lunch that one day. But they all had their own things, and you and I were wrapped up in each other."

I swallowed hard and took a bite of my sandwich, even though it tasted like sawdust. I was hungry, and I had learned to eat when I needed to. It didn't matter what it tasted like, even though I knew Sandy had made sure it was the perfect delicacy for us.

"We were all being deployed at the same time. All going to the same place, the same squadron, even though we worked in different areas. I broke my phone as soon as I landed in Virginia. I didn't know your damn number. I felt like such an idiot, but I was working my way in getting my phone back, hoping I could keep all my numbers. Soon as we landed, things went haywire. There was an explosion that had taken out six of our guys, I was working with intelligence to try to figure out the next steps. We were boots on the ground as soon as we got there, and I didn't even have time to contact my brothers, to make sure that they weren't in the explosion." I let out a breath. "Evan and Elliot were there. But it wasn't their squadron that got hit by the IED or the explosion. At least, not that time." I was grateful Bethany didn't ask anything more about that. It wasn't my story to tell, and I wasn't sure I would be able to get through it as it was.

I nearly lost my brothers countless times.

But I had lost my brothers in arms nonetheless.

"We were in a convoy heading back to the base, and I was part of base readiness. To make sure that the team was set, that we were doing what we needed to. And we were hit." My hand shook. "What turned out to be a rocket launcher hit us straight on. Took out the first four trucks, and the two behind us. The blast knocked my truck forward and onto its roof. Clayton was in the truck with me. The others were scattered around with their own people."

Flashes of memories hit me, and I swallowed hard, my mouth dry.

"It was just chance that I was with Clayton at all." I swallowed hard, trying to breathe.

"Jericho and Jennifer were in the truck in front of us, and died instantly. It took Todd two days to die. I didn't see him. I was unconscious for most of it. Clayton was still in the truck when it burned. I had been thrown out. In my dreams, I hear him screaming, but they tell me that he hadn't screamed because he died on impact. I still think maybe that they were just telling me that to make me feel better. I'm not sure, but my friends died. The four people that I counted on the most outside of my family. They died. And I got a traumatic brain injury. My brain swelled, and they thought I wasn't going to make it. There were a lot of decisions to make, and somehow Eli got to me." My lips lifted into a small smile. "My big brother got to me, and made sure that I was taken care of. He was on his way out of the military, getting ready to finish his twenty, and he got me out. He was there to make sure that I wasn't alone. That nobody had to help make those decisions when they didn't know me." I looked up at Bethany. "Because the people that knew me, who understood me, had died. But my brothers came." I shrugged, my hand shaking. "I nearly died that day, and have dealt with the ramifications ever since. And not just with the fact that I have memory loss, nausea, migraines, and a couple of seizures that made sure that I couldn't drive for the first year after I got out. I also had to deal with the families of those that died."

"What do you mean?" she asked, her eyes wide. "What do you mean?" She was so pale, and that's when I realized I was squeezing her hands so tightly that even her knuckles were white.

I let her go, but then she scrambled towards me, gripping my hands again. "Everett."

"Clayton's family won't talk to me. Todd's and Jericho's families made sure I was okay, and then cut ties." My hand shook, but she just squeezed harder. "Jennifer's dad hates me." I let out a hollow laugh as Bethany frowned.

"Why? It wasn't your fault, Everett."

"I survived. His baby girl didn't. And he knew that Jennifer and I had been a thing for like a minute in basic. It didn't matter that we were just friends, that she was brilliant and strong, and I wasn't anything more to her than just a friend. Her dad hates me because I survived and she didn't. It doesn't matter that I feel like my brain is breaking sometimes, that I am afraid I am going to lose motor functions. It doesn't matter that I can no longer do the things I did when I was in active duty. That now as the CFO of the Wilders, it's my job to deal with money and make sure we don't go bankrupt. All Jennifer's dad sees is the loser who survived."

"Everett. I'm so sorry."

She moved forward and wrapped her arms around me, hugging me tightly, and for some reason I held her right back, nearly squeezing too hard.

But I could finally breathe, just letting it out. I'd spoken about this with my brothers, of course, with my therapist because Eli made us all go. But that didn't mean I spoke about it with everybody. They didn't need to know that sometimes I passed out and that I couldn't even look at a computer screen without wanting to throw up.

This was my lot in life, my penance for surviving. I knew that, so I would live with it.

I would just hate myself a little bit more every day.

"I'm so sorry," she whispered again.

"I'm sorry, too," I said after a moment. "I'll never be the same. I'm trying to actually take care of myself so I don't hate who I am anymore, it's just taking me a while."

She met my gaze, our lunch long forgotten. For some reason, I reached forward and pushed her hair back from her face. I gently caressed her cheek, wondering what I was doing. But here she was. The woman from my dreams, the woman from my past.

I didn't even realize I was leaning down, brushing my lips against hers until I was already doing it.

She stiffened, and I leaned back and cursed under my breath.

"I'm sorry. I shouldn't have done that. You're healing, just out of a relationship. And here I am, mauling you."

"You didn't maul me. But I'm not ready, Everett. I came here, but I don't know why I came here. But thank you for trusting me with your past. With your secrets. I just, I'm sorry."

And with that, she turned and walked away, her hands tight at her side.

I made another mistake, but I didn't blame her. She

needed to walk away. She wasn't here for me. She was here because she needed a moment. Just like I had.

And I knew that even if she let me kiss her again, she would walk away no matter what.

She would leave.

She was a star. A celebrity. Everybody knew her name.

And I was just a Wilder.

Nobody.

# Chapter Seven

## Bethany

Somebody banged their fist on my door, and alarm shot through me until I remembered I was safe because I was on the Wilders' property. I would be *physically* safe, at least.

Emotionally? I didn't think safety would be an actual option.

I wasn't going to think about that at all.

"Bethany! Open up. I'm tired and I need coffee. And I need to see you."

I nearly fell off my chair as I ran towards the door, undid the locks, and threw the door open.

"Lark? What are you doing here? I didn't know you were coming!" I threw my arms around her as she hugged me tight. I inhaled that sweet floral scent that was my best friend.

Not that she always smelled like that. She liked to keep everybody on her toes and change whatever perfume she wore—some natural, some funky, anything to keep her mind going in a thousand different directions so she could find inspiration.

At least, that was what some news article had said about her at one point, and her agent went with it.

For those who knew Lark, they knew that she just wore whatever she had on hand, as long as it smelled nice.

I stepped back, looked at my strawberry-blond haired friend, and pushed that massive mane of hair away from her face.

"I cannot believe you're here." I was grinning so hard I knew my cheeks would hurt later. I just stared at her and promptly burst into tears.

My best friend kept a smile on her face as she studied mine. "Okay, I should've expected this. Let's get inside, and I will look for coffee."

I quickly wiped my tears and stepped back, using all of my training as an apparently skilled actor to make sure my tears stayed away.

"I'm sorry. Of course, let's get you coffee. I still cannot believe you're here."

Lark waved me off. "I can only be here for a day. Since it took nearly a day to travel to the states and will take another day to travel back. However, it doesn't matter. All that matters is I am here for my best friend. And you have my favorite coffee."

She moved to my espresso machine and began working all the gizmos as if she had done this a thousand times before. That was Lark. She was brilliant. She could pretty much figure out anything as long as she studied it for a minute.

Most of the time, I felt out of my depth with my best friend, just because she was so brilliant. I marveled that she had taken me in as her best friend, as I had done the same for her.

"Want me to make you something?" she asked, her hands moving with grace and experience.

"The answer is always yes when it comes to you and coffee," I answered, leaning against the doorway.

"That's what I like to hear. So...should we make a burn box or trashcan for a certain jerk? I don't know if you have any printed photos of him here, but I'm sure we could figure out a way. There's always a way when it comes to removing that memory from your brain. Because screw him." She worked confidently as she spoke, and soon we each had a latte with feather foam art on top.

I frowned. "I didn't even know that this espresso machine could foam things like that."

"It's just a setting. I can teach you."

I scowled. "I don't know if I want to learn now. I'm disgruntled."

Lark snorted, shaking her head. "Sounds about right. Now, since you burst into tears as soon as I showed up, I guess me asking if you're doing okay probably wouldn't help anything."

I took a sip of the delicious vanilla latte and sighed. "Honestly, the fact that my long-term boyfriend turned out to be cheating on me and most likely selling his side of the so-called story to the press is the least surprising thing to happen to me."

Lark took a big sip of her coffee, then set the mug down. "What on earth do you mean? I'm going to need details."

I sighed and leaned against the counter as I studied my singer-songwriter best friend. "Do you know why I'm here? Not running from the media as everybody is saying. Though perhaps that's part of it."

My best friend shook her head. "I don't. I had wondered, but I didn't want to bother you about it."

I smiled and reached out, gripping her hand. "This

is *his* place. The Wilder Retreat and Winery is his family's. It's *his*."

Lark frowned for a moment before her eyes widened and she dropped my hand. "Oh my God. Are you serious?"

I nodded. "Yes. This is his place. Him and his brothers. Everett Wilder, my one-weekend stand, a man who somehow broke my heart, lives here. I saw him here when I was at that wedding that you couldn't attend."

"I should've found a way to get here to meet him, Bethany. I'm here now. I will be meeting this jerk who never called you back."

I cringed. "There seems to have been an actual reason for that." I explained why but I didn't go into detail. It wasn't my story to tell, and the details weren't what mattered in this moment. No, it was the feeling that I hadn't been left behind. Not the way that I thought.

Lark wiped tears from her face and finished the rest of her coffee. "I'm so sorry. So, he's here, healing, with all of his brothers, and you came here as well. I assume to confront him at first, and now what are you going to do?"

I gave a hollow laugh. "That's the million-dollar question, isn't it? Because I don't know what I can do. My life is in no way ready for a relationship. Not that there would be a relationship. All he did was kiss me, and explain to me that he didn't forget me completely on purpose. That doesn't mean we have a fighting chance, or even something beyond attraction. He lives out here in Texas. I live in LA and travel all over the world all the time. And as is evidenced by my track record, being in a relationship doesn't do well with my job. I should just be alone. Honestly, I would've been better alone before all of this, but I said yes to Dallas and then never quite said no again, though I should have."

Her eyes narrowed. "He's around town with her, you know. Your nemesis."

I laughed. I couldn't help it. "My nemesis? Is that what we're calling her?"

"It's either that or we use names that I don't like to call women. But she sure likes to believe she is 'all that.' I'm sorry. I shouldn't bring it up, but that is why I'm here. Since we're not going to burn his picture in effigy or curse her with a thousand spiders, I guess you should show me around the resort. I could use some relaxation time."

Guilt filled me. "You shouldn't have to travel all the way out here in what I think is your only free time right now. I'm so proud of this tour and everything that comes with it, but you must be exhausted. You shouldn't have come."

Lark narrowed her eyes before waving me off. "When I broke my leg on stage, and nobody was around me except for my former team, who flew to me? You. Who held my hand when I cried and had to get back on stage and pretend that I didn't have pins in my leg? You. Who held my hand when my former producer decided that he liked it better when I was on my knees instead of singing? You. Who has been with me through every up and down of my career? *You.* We are best friends for a reason. Because we are always there for each other. So yes, I might sleep on the plane and be exhausted later, but who cares? We only get one life, Bethany. I'm living it. So don't forget that."

Tears filled my eyes again, and I looked at my best friend. "It has been a weird few months. And I hate that everything that you've gone through seems never-ending."

"I would say ditto, but I think you understand that."

I knew Lark was far more tired than she let on, for more reasons than just travel, but we each had our own demons, so I let her pretend that all was well.

"I have a few scripts to go over later, but why don't we go get lunch at the restaurant at the main building, and maybe I can introduce you around." At the gleam in her eyes, I shook my head. "I meant meet the girls and team here. Maybe a Wilder, but not on purpose."

I laughed at the look on her face and knew that this was probably a bad idea. Because Everett wasn't mine, he had never truly been. I'd had a crush, a moment of weakness. But I shouldn't rely on those feelings. I knew better than anyone that they could lie. That acting was one way to make things work.

I acted every day. I didn't need to act in life as well.

I quickly cleaned myself up so I looked presentable. Lark did the same, considering she just got off a long plane ride. And then, arm in arm, we laughed and skipped our way towards the restaurant. We wore hats and sunglasses, even though they didn't really hide who we were. Nobody paid us much attention, and I was grateful for that. Most people were here for an upcoming wedding and relaxation.

And while my heart was a bruise, my pride shaken, I was finding time to breathe, something I wasn't good at these days. But I was doing what my manager and agent both said, finding a way to relax.

So here I was, finding that way.

"Bethany!" Alexis said as she opened the door to the restaurant. "I was just coming to steal you."

The other woman's eyes widened as she looked over at my companion before she schooled her features, doing her best not to reveal she had recognized Lark.

"Hi, Alexis. Meet my friend Lark. She's here for just a day, sadly, but she wanted to visit."

"Oh, that's wonderful. You should have let us know you were coming! We would've made sure you had your own cabin welcome basket. Or anything that you need. Seriously, just let us know if you want us to make that happen now."

"Bethany said you all were amazing over here. I guess I should say 'y'all.'"

"We are very good with the 'y'all's here. Seriously though, the girls and I were going to do a wine and dine lunch over at the winery. Would you like to join us?" she asked, and I looked over at Lark, who nodded.

"You said wine and dine. I'm excited about that." Then she looked at her closely. She was wearing soft linen pants and a cropped top, her hair flowing out from underneath the hat. "Am I dressed okay for it?"

Alexis grinned. "You look amazing. And this is just a private event in the employees' lounge area at the winery. It'll just be myself, Maddie, our wine club manager, and Kendall, our chef. Although she's pregnant and won't be drinking the wine, she will be providing food. But we have to make sure she doesn't eat soft cheeses. She keeps trying to sneak them, and I think Evan will ground us all if I let her eat brie."

"I think we can stop her. Maybe. She does seem kinda strong," I said with a laugh.

"It's true. She could take any of us. Joy is also coming, Elijah's girlfriend." Alexis let out a soft laugh. "And I just realized I'm naming a bunch of people you might have met, but most likely not. Elijah is my brother-in-law. Joy is our friend. Naomi will be in and out since she's on duty today, but we wanted to ensure she could enjoy herself a bit today." She looked between us. "She's our innkeeper. You met her when Eli first got you signed in."

I nodded. "Oh yes, I remember her. She was growling at that big, bearded man."

Alexis threw her head back and laughed. "That would be Amos. Our winery manager. If they're not growling at each other, then I'd be worried."

That made me snort. "Wine and lunch sound amazing. Thank you for thinking of us."

"Of course. I should mention that we do have a wedding later this afternoon, and there will be photographers around. I want you guys to feel safe, and that you can go everywhere around our property, but that is the reality of what happens when you have a wedding. I will be in and out for that because they didn't use me as the wedding planner." She rolled her eyes, and my own eyes widened.

"Is that not your job? I'm sorry, that was too forward."

"No, it's fine. They scheduled with the Wilders the first year they were open, and then had to postpone for a couple of years for various reasons. I don't know the full of it, but they refused to work with the plan. They wanted to do things their way and their own package. Which is fine, because that's the contract that they signed, but it's making my other brother-in-law want to pull out his hair." She let out a breath. "And that would be Elliot, the baby brother. But don't tell him I said that. And that was way too much information for you."

Lark blinked. "Wait, how many brothers-in-law do you have? Do they all begin with the letter E?"

Alexis grinned. "I am married to a lovely man named Eli Wilder. And he has five brothers and a sister, all with the letter E. I do not know what their parents were thinking. I've yet to get all of their names right throughout the day. I'm pretty sure they even get their own names wrong."

We giggled and followed her through the employee entrance towards a golf cart.

"Now, I will get you over to the winery in my fancy golf cart, if you don't mind. We could walk, but I'd rather get started sooner than later." She winked as she said it, and Lark and I jumped into the cart and made our way over to the winery.

The area was gorgeous, the sun overhead but not too hot. The sky was blue, not a cloud in it. I thought it would be lovely for a wedding, though I did find it weird that they didn't want an actual wedding planner with them. But what did I know, I was used to other people planning things for me. And I had no clue how to plan a wedding at all.

Not that I was ever going to get married.

The media and paparazzi were enough as it was with just the break up. I didn't even want to think about what would happen with a divorce. Not that I thought all marriages led to divorce, but I wasn't quite sure I believed in marriage anymore.

Lark elbowed me in the side, and I pushed those thoughts out of my mind. It wasn't that she could read my mind, but I was pretty sure my best friend knew where my thoughts had gone.

We pulled up to the winery, and I inhaled the sweet scent of the Texas air, then promptly sneezed, my best friend laughing at me.

"You know you have allergies. You should know better than to go around just sniffing the air with all the cedar out there."

Alexis winced and held back a laugh, leading us

towards the back employee area. "Believe me, I'm on three kinds of allergy medications, because I'm allergic to the state I've lived in for most of my life. You can take off your hat and glasses, by the way. It'll just be us back here. Unless you like them. I just don't want you to feel like you have to hide."

I did as she said, grateful. "Doesn't keep our identity secret or anything, but it does help a little. People don't automatically recognize us, as long as we aren't making too big of a commotion. We can usually get from place to place without constant attention."

"We are doing our best to keep you under the radar here, but other guests have phones."

"You have a wonderful place here. And I was grateful that I had called your husband ahead of time so that way I could make it through security." She winked as she said it, and I nearly tripped over my own feet along with Alexis.

"Eli knew you would be here, and he didn't tell me?" she gasped.

"Don't get him in trouble. I wanted to be a surprise. And I wanted to make sure I wasn't going to screw up security."

Alexis nodded. "He normally keeps me up to date with what's going on, and I appreciate that. But I am going to have to go growl at my husband. Mostly, because he likes it when I do."

She blushed, and I smiled, thinking of the two of them. They were perfectly in love. I saw the way that they smiled at each other and how neither one of them backed down for the other. But they did bend when needed.

I wanted that. Or, at least, I thought I did. I wasn't sure what I wanted anymore.

We made our way to the back room where food, wine, and people were already about. Kendall stood beside the cheese board, her hands on her belly, as a woman with long hair pulled away from her face scowled and pushed her back.

"Oh, no you don't. You should be sitting down with your feet up. I will bring food to you, but no cheese."

Kendall scowled and stomped her way to her chair. As she sat down, another woman came and put her feet up, and Kendall sighed.

"Why am I so moody? My friends are taking care of me, I shouldn't be growly. But all I want is soft cheese. And I don't even *like* soft cheese. What is wrong with me?" She looked up as she finished speaking and blushed.

"Oh. Hi, Bethany. And oh my God, you're Lark

Thornbird." Kendall put her hand over her mouth. "Sorry," she mumbled.

Lark waved it off. "You must be Kendall. The famous chef I've heard so much about."

"I am going to write that on my business card now. I can't believe *the* Lark Thornbird is going to eat my food." She looked at me. "Not that having Bethany Cole eat my food wasn't an amazing thing, but now there's both of you. I think my heart is racing."

I laughed, then went to squeeze Kendall's hand. "I've eaten your food before. You had an entire wedding filled to the brim with A-list stars. You should be used to it. Your food is some of the best we've had."

"And now I'm going to cry."

Alexis moved forward and handed her a tissue. "You're fine. Be good for the babies."

"Babies? Twins?" Lark's eyes widened.

"Yes! Why am I nervous?" Kendall asked with a laugh, as others joined in on her laughter.

"I am so freaking nervous because two of my favorite people are about to taste our wine," another woman said as she went forward and held out her hand. "Hi! I'm Maddie."

"It's nice to meet you," Lark said.

"You have written some of my favorite songs. I just

want to put that out there before I act normal," the final woman in the room said as she came forward. "I'm Joy."

"It's so great to meet all of you. And I'm glad that my music is some of your favorite. And I'm never normal, so don't worry about it."

Lark did what she did best, put people at ease. Soon we were all sitting down, drinking wine, and eating delicious canapés and appetizers. Kendall had a food plate of her own and was drinking out of her large bottle of water.

Kendall had to get up often to pee, but the girls kept her hydrated. I couldn't help but think about how these women were a family, even if only two of them were technically related, and that was through marriage.

They were brilliant, secure in their jobs and femininity, and three of them were in love with Wilder brothers. I didn't know Maddie's story, and she didn't seem to be connected to any of the men, but for all I knew she was secretly dating one of the other Wilders I had met.

As long as it wasn't Everett, it didn't matter to me. And at that moment, I knew I'd probably had too much wine. My head spun. If I was being territorial about Everett, it meant I needed to stop drinking.

But then Alexis filled my glass again, and I continued to drink and let myself finally relax with women I felt like I could trust, though I didn't trust most people.

I didn't tend to have more than a single glass when I was with people I didn't know. Or even people I did know, for that matter. I needed to be in control no matter what. One wrong photo of me sitting next to an empty bottle of wine, and suddenly I was an alcoholic with a problem and would lose my job. That was the cost of my life, the cost of my success.

And I was learning the hard way that no matter what I did, sometimes I would fail.

Case in point, the news article that flashed on Maddie's phone as she walked by.

**Dallas and Cassandra, living the life of lovers. Lonely Bethany in seclusion.**

I scowled and finished my glass of wine in one gulp as Maddie looked down at her phone and cursed.

"I have major news set as alerts on my phone because I need to for this job. I don't know why people think lies like this are major news. I'm sorry that you had to see that." She swiped away the notification and flipped off her phone, and I couldn't help but chuckle with her and the others.

"It's fine. The media's going to say what they want about me. And they're most likely going to be wrong. I just hate the fact that he's out there with the woman that he's been cheating on me with, the woman that constantly puts me down in the media and has been my nemesis for who knows how long, and he can do no wrong. While I am hiding and licking my wounds. I don't even fucking love him."

I quickly set down my glass, as if it was a snake that hissed at me, and shook my head. "And that's enough of that."

"I'm glad you finally said the words that have been whirling within me this whole time," Lark put in, setting down her empty glass. "Good for you. Fuck Dallas. Just don't *fuck* him because you know he wasn't a good lay."

The other women burst out laughing, and I had no idea why I felt so safe with them. I had just said the absolutely wrong thing that could get me in trouble in so many circles, and yet they loved it. And I trusted them.

This was probably going to bite me in the ass later.

"What do you mean, your nemesis?" Maddie leaned forward. "You do not need to talk about it if you don't want to."

I sighed and let Alexis pour me another glass of wine. She was going to be my downfall, if Everett wasn't first. "Cassandra Fox and I have always gone for the same parts since we started. I kept getting them, and she didn't. So, every time that we would go to an event, she would make sure that she figured out what I was wearing, and wear something like it, but better. At least in her eyes. Or if I was going out to a certain lunch, or even just out with friends, she would make sure she was there, dressed to the nines, and ensure the paparazzi was alerted. I couldn't go shopping or out to an eatery without her showing up. She was always there. She has spies everywhere, and she does it not only to me, but others, too."

"I hate her," Lark mumbled.

"I hate her, too, and not just because of that. She's a terrible actress," Joy said, scowling. "And she always puts others down when she's trying to lift herself up. That's not what you do with other women. There are enough crowns for everyone."

I lifted my glass in toast. "To crowns."

"To crowns," everyone echoed, as Kendall laughed.

"You guys are trashed, and I love you. And I am a little jealous. However, I am falling asleep, so I did something you're all going to hate me for."

I narrowed my eyes. "What did you do?"

"Nothing that's going to get you in trouble. However, I did call the men."

And with that, the Wilder brothers walked in.

They were like six sexy, bearded, hot as fuck Greek gods as they walked in, and actual wind from the ceiling fan blowing some of their hair from their faces. It was as if they had just walked off a rugged runway, and my mouth watered.

Of course, it was only for one man.

"Well, the women are drunk. This is going to be fun," Evan Wilder grumbled.

He went directly to his wife and helped her out of the chair. "You okay, baby?" he asked. That big, growly, stone-faced man melted for his wife.

My eyes filled with tears, and the room swayed. Or maybe I did.

Yeah, I'd had too much wine.

Eli went to Alexis, kissed her hard on the mouth, then lifted her into his arms. "Okay, baby. It looks like you had fun. At least I see there are notes for the wine, so you did some work."

"We had fun. And I might've had a drink."

He laughed and carried his wife out as I leaned against my chair, only a little jealous.

"Okay, Bethany. Let's get you to your cabin."

I blinked. "Everett? You're not my husband."

Somebody snorted behind him, but he ignored it. "Let me get you safely home. I didn't think you drank."

"It's not safe to. This place makes me feel safe."

His eyes softened and I let him lift me into his arms. He cradled me to his chest and I wrapped my arms around his neck. "I can't let anyone see me like this."

The reality was slowly starting to settle in, my body going cold.

"I have the car parked around the back, tinted windows and all. Nobody's going to see you. I promise. You're safe with me, Bethany."

And the thing was, I believed him.

Out of the corner of my eye, I saw Elijah taking care of Joy, and one of the other brothers, I thought maybe Elliot, helping Maddie. Another brother stuffed Lark in the back of the SUV beside me, but I didn't know which one that was. East?

They buckled me in, and Lark and I cuddled into each other as we were driven to the cabin. This was probably a mistake, but drunk Bethany didn't care.

I let Everett carry me inside, safe from prying eyes, and I noticed that the final Wilder brought Lark inside.

"I hear you have a flight tomorrow. Hopefully, it's in the afternoon."

"It is. What's your name?" my best friend asked.

"I'm East. Now, do I need to tuck you in? Because I don't know how to do that. I'll get you some water, though. And aspirin. Because it is going to hurt tomorrow."

"I don't get hangovers. I have a decent constitution." Lark sounded sober now, and I frowned, a little jealous.

"Whatever. You're still getting water."

"Are all the Wilders grumpy? Or just you?"

"You'll never know. Now, get some sleep. Thanks for taking care of our girl."

I have no idea what he meant by that because Everett was tucking me into bed, and I was wiggling out of my pants.

He groaned, and I smiled up at him.

"I'm drunk."

"Yes, you are. I'm going to get you water and aspirin, too."

"I shouldn't be drunk."

"You needed to take some time for yourself. I'm glad you and the girls had fun."

"I missed you, Everett," I said as I leaned against the pillow, not even sure I was speaking aloud anymore.

He sighed and the sound hurt my heart. "I wish you missed me when you were awake," he whispered.

Or maybe I was just imagining that, too.

And perhaps I was only imagining the feel of his lips against my forehead as he walked away.

I closed my eyes and let the wine take me under.

# Chapter Eight

## Everett

The numbers flew across the screen, my gaze a laser on them. At least that's what I liked to imagine what I looked like when I was working. I sat in my office, my coffee cold beside my keyboard, my water bottle full. I needed to get through a few more calculations and projections, and then I would be ready for our family meeting.

I was the chief financial officer of our place. After complicated issues stemming from the winery side a year ago, it was nice to see that we were finally fully in the black again after losing so many barrels of wine to the Dodges' sabotage.

It set my teeth on edge to think about how much we had lost, not just monetarily, because of somebody else's greed and decisions.

But we were headed towards a good year and had a wonderful batch of grapes, according to Amos and the rest of the team.

I wasn't great with wine. I barely knew the difference between a Pinot Noir and a Cabernet. All I knew was that my drink was in front of me, and I gave what I felt were decent descriptions of the flavors. My brothers had wanted everybody's opinion on what they thought tasted good, because not everybody was going to come in with a complicated or enhanced palate.

Apparently, I was the "everyday wine drinker." In other words, I preferred beer. But I wasn't going to tell my brothers that.

I smiled, thinking that a beer sounded really good right then.

Too bad we hadn't opened a brewery like our friend Roy up near Austin. But then we would've ended up competing against one another because we were so close travel-wise, so the winery had been perfect. This place had been ready-made. We'd settled in and made it wilder. Pun intended.

I wasn't quite sure how I had ended up as the CFO of the company. I'd always been good with numbers, so maybe that was part of it. I had handled the family accounting throughout the years.

Even though taxes for single military guys weren't too complicated, it was easier if I just did them all for everybody. And cheaper. That had turned into projections and wanting to make sure we were all set up for our retirements. And now here I was, partly in charge of a multimillion-dollar company, and it still didn't feel real.

If I kept thinking about work and wine, I wouldn't think about the fact that I had tucked Bethany into bed the night before. I had tried not to listen to her sweet words. Because, of course, she had just been drunk. It hadn't been her true thoughts.

"Hello there, brother, are you headed to the meeting?"

I looked up to see Elijah in his suit and grinned. "Did you have a meeting with the Bliss brothers today?"

Elijah shrugged. "Yes, and I thought I looked damn good in the suit because Joy drooled at it, so I kept it on."

That made me laugh.

"At least you are not subtle about it. It does look good on you."

"Well, thank you. You should wear your suits."

I looked down at my button-down shirt and suit pants. "I'm sort of dressed up. You know we could wear jeans here and Eli wouldn't care."

"Like I care about what Eli thinks," Elijah said with a roll of his eyes. "Come on. Grab your tablet and whatever else you need, and let's go. The kitchen catered for us again, and I'm starving."

"You're always hungry." I rubbed my temples. I stood up, and my brother's gaze narrowed.

"Headache?"

I nodded and then looked at my phone and did the math. "I can take something, but first I'm going to drink some water. It's better for me to try to hydrate first."

"If you say so. But you probably need food as well. I see you only finished half of your coffee. So you probably didn't even think about finishing breakfast."

"You're right. But I finished my work, and I am trying to do better."

It was a common refrain.

I got my water bottle and my tablet and followed Elijah to the conference room.

We were all set in the main building, with most of our offices here. East even had an office here, though he never used it. Evan's and Elijah's offices were in the winery area because that's where they worked.

My office was next door to Eli's, but my brother was

already in the conference room, along with everyone else.

We rented this room out to companies who came here for retreats and other events. We booked it once a week for us, sometimes more, because it was nice to see everybody in person. Sometimes, if Elijah was out of town on a scouting trip, or if Eli was at a conference or something along with Elliot, they came in through video chat, but we tried to meet in person as much as possible.

We even forced our sister to join in, even though she wasn't part of the company. But she was a Wilder at heart, too, and liked to know what we were doing, and usually had good insight.

Maddie, Kendall, and Alexis were already there, since they worked with major parts of the company, and while only two of them were Wilders by marriage, we all worked together and had part of the presentation to go through.

"Oh good, you're here," Alexis said. "Go eat."

I narrowed my gaze at her. "Elijah text you as we were walking here?"

Eli came up behind her and narrowed his gaze. "No, but if he's on your case, I will be too. Go eat, drink some water. I can see that vein at your temple pulsing."

I flipped him off, and Maddie clicked her tongue.

"Excuse me. We are in a place of business. I do not appreciate that type of language, verbal or nonverbal."

I snorted and rolled my eyes. "Wasn't it you that screamed 'shit' really loudly when you stubbed your toe, and I had to cough so nobody heard?"

Maddie blushed. "Stop it. You said you wouldn't tell."

"Now, Maddie, are you really cursing in front of guests?" Elijah asked, teasing.

Maddie's face closed up. "I would never do that, Mr. Wilder."

Then she stomped away, and I looked at Elijah, who just shrugged.

"I don't know. She's been in a mood."

I winced, since I knew better than to say phrases like that in front of any of our family.

We all got to work, and I ate and drank water like I was supposed to, all under the watchful gazes of my family.

I worried about them as much as they worried about me, but I guess I just didn't like to be in the hot seat.

"By the way, the cousins called," Eli put in as we were finishing up our meeting.

"From your dad's side of the family?" Kendall asked, her hand on her stomach.

"Wait. There are more Wilders out there?" Maddie asked, her eyes wide.

I snorted. "Yes, there are more Wilders, not just us."

"Well, that's not altogether reassuring," she said with a laugh as Alexis and Kendall both high-fived her.

"What do they want?" East asked, speaking up for the first time during the entire meeting.

Eli shrugged. "Their dad is thinking about doing a family reunion, meaning we would have to show up. It's been how long since we've seen them? I don't know."

"Have him call me. I can handle our end," Elliot put in, tapping his pen. "It's what I do."

Relieved, because I knew Elliot could handle it, I nodded, and we moved on to the next point of the meeting.

Evan was saying something that was probably important, but I glanced at my phone and saw an email that took all my attention.

I quickly tucked it away, my stomach rolling. I didn't want to see Jennifer's father's name. But there it was, in black-and-white. Bold and underlined and unread.

I didn't need to see any more accusations and hate. At least not now.

The meeting ended soon after that, and I cleaned up my mess and set my things back in my office, practically running out of the building because I needed air.

The sky was a bit hazy, dust and clouds taking over the day, but it still felt a little fresher than anything inside.

I walked into the garden area between the two buildings, and just strolled down the stone path, trying to focus, to breathe.

Everything hurt, and I hated myself for it because the guilt was there. It always was.

I turned the corner towards one of the many fountains on the property, and there she was.

As if I had been drawn to her. My North Star, my homing beacon.

Maybe that was always the case when it came to Bethany.

She looked up when I came to her. She set down the book she was reading. "Everett. I didn't know you'd be here."

I smiled at her, the tension still riding me, but this time for a whole new reason. "I just needed some air. I can go another way to give you space."

She met my gaze and I was afraid I'd said the wrong thing, then she patted the seat on the bench next to her. "Come sit down. I'm still hungover and feel like a dork."

I smiled at the large water bottle next to her, toasted hers with mine.

"I'm glad that you're at least up and about. Is Lark gone?" I asked, sitting next to her.

"She is. I'm sad. I wish we had more time to spend together. She's in the busy part of her season, so soon as the tour is over and she gets back to writing, maybe I can force her to stay with me for a bit."

"You should. You brighten when she's around."

She smiled at me, studying my face. "That's a kind thing to say. She's my best friend. Now, what's wrong, Everett? I might be hungover, but you look worse than me."

"Thanks for that," I said with a laugh. "Jennifer's dad emailed me. I haven't read it yet. I don't know if I want to. But I feel like I need to."

I hadn't meant to blurt the words out, but then they were just there. It was so easy to talk to her, even when it wasn't.

She frowned, her eyes intense. She reached forward and hugged me tightly. "I'm sorry."

"It's not your fault." I hugged her back, inhaling that sweet scent of hers.

"It's not your fault either," she whispered.

I froze for an instant, then pulled away slightly. She looked up at me, her mouth parting.

I lowered my head to hers and brushed my lips against hers, like we had been doing this a thousand times, over a thousand years. I didn't mean to do it, I truly didn't. It was just so natural.

She closed her eyes and I deepened the kiss, my tongue brushing against hers.

I pulled away and winced. "I'm sorry."

She smiled softly, but I couldn't read the expression in her gaze. "No, Everett. I like your kisses."

I froze, not sure I heard her correctly. "You do?"

"Of course, I do. That was never the problem. I'm just, I'm not a good bet right now, Everett."

I laughed, though there was no humor in it. "I'm not either." Then I kissed her again.

I couldn't help it, it's what I'd wanted to do from the first moment I saw her again, even when I hadn't even remembered her.

I cupped her face, her skin soft and smooth under my touch. She slid her hands down my chest, her fingers twining with the fabric, before I pulled away, my breath coming in pants.

"I should probably stop doing that, just in case someone comes by."

She froze and looked around, her eyes widening. "I didn't even think about that. Damn it, Everett. You make my mind go haywire. I can't let anyone take a photo of you kissing me like that. You don't want your face all over the news."

I brushed her hair back from her eyes and swallowed hard. "Let me make you dinner. I know we can't go out in public. It wouldn't be good for you, or anything like that. I want to kiss you again, Bethany. Even if we only have these few stolen moments."

I was so afraid she was going to say no. I knew she would. That was inevitable.

She was Bethany Cole

She was everything. And I was a Wilder.

She touched my cheek, then let her hand fall. "The answer should be no."

I froze at the word *should*.

"But?"

"But yes, I'd love to have dinner with you. Even if we both know it's a mistake."

Relief slammed into me and I smiled.

I might not know what I was doing, but at least I was going full force into it.

Because Bethany Cole had just said yes.

Thank God.

# Chapter Nine

### Bethany

"The studio is excited about the next phase. I know that you're working with your trainer through video messaging, but as soon as you get back, we're going to have to start the next steps."

I nodded at my agent and remembered that she couldn't see me. "No problem. I'm a sweaty mess right now since I just ran five miles and then did strength training. I need to shower and get ready for the day, but yes, I'm excited too. I feel stronger than I did before, and not just physically."

I could hear the smile in my agent's voice as she

spoke. "That's good. You needed this rest. Even though I'm forcing you to work out and remain in shape for your action movie."

I laughed. "I love doing these, even though going back to the high-protein diet so I can pretend I have abs of steel isn't my idea of fun."

"You don't need abs of steel. We can just have them photoshop abs on later if you want."

"No, we are not photoshopping abs on me. I'm going to be fit. I'm not going to show off a body that is fake. There has to be a middle ground, and I'm going to find it. I have hips. I'm always going to have hips. And curves. Maybe not the same curves I would have if I didn't work out as much as I do for this role, but I'm not a size zero, and I never have been."

"I know. And I've never wanted you to be anything less than you are. And the studio wants you to be who you are. You just have to be in shape so you can keep running around a lot like they have you doing."

I started, knowing that my agent was on the same page with me regarding my personal body image, mental health, and the way I fit in with these movies. I did films that were considered Oscar bait by some people. Movies where I threw myself emotionally into the role, so much so in fact that I did the same physically. And then I did action movies where I needed to be in shape to keep up with the stunt doubles. I was running and jumping for hours a day, and having dialogue while I was ducking out of the way of imaginary magic balls of light. I needed to be in shape for that, and not because of what other people thought I should look like. Oh they might try and force me into that, but I wasn't going to let them. I stood on the shoulders of others who had done the work, who had pushed boundaries set on them by people who didn't understand. So I was going to continue to lift when I needed to. Even if some people thought it was just for this silly action movie that gave them laughs and tears. I did it for many reasons, but part of that was for my own health.

"Did you look over the last script I gave you?" she asked, as I was thinking through my thoughts about my own worth.

"I did. It's okay. But I don't feel the motivation of the third act for my character."

"That's what I thought. Send me over your notes, and I'll see what I can do. I don't know if this is the completed script or if there are rewrites to come. If you're not feeling it, we will find something else. I have stacks upon stacks of offers for you. And since everything is hot right now, let's use it."

"You mean, use the fact that I'm in the news because Dallas dumped me?"

"I was going to say use whatever we could because you are an amazing actress, but sure. Screw Dallas. You know his little problem is going to get him into more trouble than he thinks. He's just one step away from having it all blow up in his face. People aren't going to want to work with a man who is unreliable. And he showed the world he wasn't reliable, even if they don't realize it yet."

"I'm glad you're on my side with this, but I still feel like he's gotten away with so much."

"It won't last. You are strong, you're talented. And when you show up hot on your first red carpet post-breakup, you will be hotter than ever, with the pride and power that comes with who you are. The media will get it. And if they don't, the next starlet will fall, and this drama will be forgotten. That's Hollywood."

"I don't know if that was a warning or pep talk. Or how I'm supposed to feel about that," I said after a minute.

"I don't know where I was going with that, other than that you are talented and one of my favorite people in the world. We're going to get you as many jobs as you want. Because they're out there, and they want you. Just use this time to breathe, because you won't have much time to breathe soon."

"I guess that is a good thing."

I let out a breath and listened to a few more work things before I finally hung up and went to shower and get ready for my date.

A date with Everett Wilder.

I didn't know how it had come about.

I was oddly nervous, though I shouldn't be. I had gone out on dates before, and some of the dates had even been with Everett himself. And yet, this was different. Everything was different. Because I wasn't the same person I had been, and neither was he.

And that might be why I was so damn nervous. It was all I could do not to be nauseous or end up with shakes.

I should've said no. I should have walked away and not let him kiss me again. Well, that's a copout. Because I kissed him right back. I shouldn't blame him for my own desires. Just because I had no idea what the hell I was doing didn't mean it was Everett's fault.

I quickly studied myself in the mirror, running my hands over my soft dove-gray dress. I hadn't brought much with me in terms of clothes for this impromptu retreat. I could've gone anywhere in the world, but I had come to the Wilders', and now I was going on a date with one of them. A secret date, because we didn't want the press over the world to know about it. I couldn't keep my own affairs safe, so perhaps I could try to keep his.

It was a simple gray cotton dress that went to mid-thigh and wrapped slightly around my chest, giving me decent cleavage. I was comfortable but still cute.

I wasn't very good at this whole dating thing, as evidenced by my relationship with Dallas. I'm pretty sure I only really remained with him for so long because it was easier than walking away. It was easier to let the media and studios wonder what we were doing together rather than wondering who got dumped.

Now I was living with that, still fielding calls from countless people who wanted to know more and wanted more of me.

I was still thinking about what all of that meant and what I was supposed to do, but I was grateful my team was good at keeping me safe. However, I knew the bubble of privacy was going to pop any minute. I would have to leave the Wilders and find another place to hide.

Though I hated the word *hide*; I never wanted to use it again.

I slid my feet into my heels, tousled my hair a bit, and figured that would have to do. I didn't look like I was ready for lunch on Rodeo Drive or even a press call, but I thought I looked nice.

Yet I was still nervous about what Everett would think.

The doorbell rang on the small cottage, and I

frowned, wondering who that could be. I thought I was meeting Everett at his cabin, but maybe I had gotten it wrong.

I grabbed my bag, went to the door, and froze at the sight of him in gray slacks and a white shirt.

"Hi there. I realize that we were going to have you come to me, but then I figured if this was a date outside of our Wilder compound, I would come to pick you up. So I wanted this to be all normal." He swallowed hard, and I watched the long, lean lines of his throat work. "You look edible."

I blushed, shaking my head. "That's what you're going with? Edible? I kind of like it. Although if any other man said that to me, I would walk away."

He laughed, and I was grateful he understood. "Oh, I get you. Any other man called you edible, and there would be a fight on our hands, but no, you're edible just because of who you are. And I feel like that made no sense."

"Not really, but I still like you. Dinner at your place still?" I asked, still nervous.

He nodded. "Yes, I'm going to make it while you're there, so I have everything prepped. That way, I didn't leave the stove on or anything when I was gone."

It was hard to focus when he was around, and maybe that was a problem. "I guess that makes sense."

"Come on. Let's go."

I slid my hand into his after locking the door, and then he jumped into his golf cart, laughing at the absurdity of the situation.

He had been joking when he called it a compound earlier, but he wasn't wrong. The place was a compound. I felt safe here, safe in a way I hadn't felt before. And I didn't think it had anything to do with the security measures they had taken.

No, it was all to do with the man beside me.

Safety and danger all wrapped up into one very delectable package.

As soon as we got inside, he poured me a glass of white wine, and I watched as he began dinner, the big pot on the stove filled with water, near-boiling.

"I heated the water to boiling before I left, then shut it off, so it shouldn't take too long. We're having scallop and shrimp scampi."

My stomach grumbled. "Oh my. That sounds amazing. And two of my favorite things."

He met my gaze, and I saw something there I didn't want to name.

"I remember. The recipe is Kendall's. So hopefully I don't screw it up."

"Let me help. I'm not saying that you can't do it on your own, but I don't like to just stand here and watch."

"We can do that. Do you want to make the salad? I have vegetables and possibly dressing." He blinked. "I should have dressing. I was going to check, but then I forgot. Busy day, and I had a headache."

Worry hit me, and I looked over at him. "You okay?"

He waved off my worry. "I am. But I had to do my deep breathing exercises and take a minute to rest, just like they told me to do, and that meant I was behind. I'm fine now. I promise."

"If you're sure. I'm still going to worry about you."

He met my gaze, the understanding there touching me. "I'm still going to worry about you, too. It's what we do."

I searched his fridge for the salad ingredients, pulled out his vegetables, and then saw a half-empty bottle of ranch that I figured was expired.

I held back a roll of my eyes and then made my way to his pantry and nodded. I pulled out lemon juice, olive oil, champagne vinegar, and a few other seasonings and set to work on making my own dressing.

"I have no idea what you're doing." Everett shook his head, his lips twitching.

"I'm making dressing because your ranch is expired."

"That just shows you I don't eat salads. And while I

like ranch with my pizza and wings, I'm usually at one of my brothers' houses."

"It's fine. I started you a grocery list and took care of the ranch."

"What would I do without you?" he asked, teasing, before he kissed me softly.

That was a problem. I would have to walk away, and so would he. But I could have fun in this moment. I needed to remember that.

I quickly tossed a salad together as he added our white wine to the scampi and did the little flip thing with the saucepan that always did things to my insides.

"I've no idea why that's so hot."

"I know you're not just talking about the flames. However, it's the forearms." He winked as he said it. He looked down at his arms which made me do the same thing.

And, with his sleeves rolled up, I could indeed see his forearms, the ink tattooed there, the strong muscles that made my mouth water. "Watch this."

And then he did that little flip again, the shrimp and scallops floating through the air for a second before they settled back down into the sauce. Yet I only really watched that part for moments. My eyes were transfixed on the smooth muscle and the way that I remembered how he'd use that strength of his to hold me against the wall, slowly working in and out of me until both of us came.

"Okay then," I said as I gulped some wine, telling myself not to press my thighs together.

He winked at me and then sipped his wine. "My mouth is suddenly parched."

"Stop trying to turn me on with the shrimp."

"I didn't know I could do that. It's kind of sexy."

"Shrimp is never sexy."

"Then you've never seen me eat a shrimp cocktail."

I rolled my eyes, sipped my wine, and went to stand next to him at the stove.

"It looks delicious. Kendall is a great chef."

"Ouch. I'm right here. Doing all the work. Slowly looking through her recipe to make sure I didn't mess up anything stupid. Like forget to add the pasta."

"The pasta looks to be right where it should be. My mouth is watering."

"Good." He winced. "Shit, I forgot. Sandy made some crusty bread for us with salted butter. The French way."

My mouth watered, and I followed his directions as he told me where everything was. Soon, we were sitting at his kitchen table, dipping crusty French bread into French butter or olive oil. Adding Parmesan to our salads as we ate and talked, the shrimp and scallop scampi cooked to perfection.

"I honestly didn't know you could cook like this."

"I really can't. Kendall puts out perfect instructions. Without her? I can't do anything."

"I'm glad that your brother married her then."

"I'm glad that he married again."

I frowned. "They were married before? Wait. I knew that."

"It's a very long story that I can't get into. And it's almost as interesting as the story about the time that Eli and Alexis met for the first time."

"Oh?" I asked, nearly licking my plate as I finished my meal.

"You see, they met underneath the moonlight at a dance at a wedding, and then she said yes to another man when he proposed to her right there."

I blinked. "Excuse me? That seems like the wrong ending to a movie."

"Tell me about it. And then she came to work here, and here we are, with more women as Wilders than ever. It's been nice for Eliza, our sister. She was outnumbered for way too long."

"I would think so."

"My parents, God rest their souls, somehow raised seven kids, after being weird and naming us all with the same letter, and yet our paths were remarkably similar even though I don't think we planned it."

"You joined the military right out of high school?"

"I did. There wasn't a lot of money for college, and while I could've gone to trade school, and maybe should have, I wanted to follow in my brother's footsteps. So I did. It didn't work out exactly how I wanted, but I don't think that's the case for most people who make decisions when they're seventeen. But I got to meet some of the best people in my life. Even for a short time."

I reached out and gripped his hand. "They were wonderful. For the moments I knew them, I could tell they were wonderful."

He smiled softly, then cleared his throat. "Let's clean up our dishes. No more talk about sad things. Tonight is a date. This was to woo you." He smacked a hard kiss on my lips and then picked up my dishes and I nodded, knowing that he needed this moment too.

All we seemed to do was talk about serious things and everything that was wrong with us. Everything that would and should pull us apart.

So tonight we wouldn't. Tonight, we'd just pretend. And it's what I needed.

We did the dishes together, our hands sliding against one another as we sank them into the hot soapy water.

Soon his arms were wrapped around me and I was pressed against the counter.

"Dishes as foreplay? I never would've thought."

"Oh, I've been thinking."

He kissed me again, and I was grateful that I was holding onto the counter, even with wet hands. He knelt in front of me, the rough calluses on his fingers an erotic caress against my thighs. When he slid his hands up my dress, over my butt, and tugged on the sides of my panties, I groaned, letting my thighs spread just ever so slightly.

"That's my girl. Always eager. Always wanting. I missed this."

Then he shoved his head up my skirt, the sensation and view nearly sending me over the edge. He blew a cool breath over my panties before sliding them down my thighs so slowly that each touch of silk and lace against my skin racked my nerve endings.

He helped me step out of my panties, still in my heels, and then he shoved my dress up over my hips, the cool air of the kitchen and the warm breath escaping his lips fighting for dominance along the bare skin of my pussy.

"I think I found my perfect dessert. All swollen and ready for my mouth. Are you going to come on my face,

Bethany? Will you let me taste and suck on this sweet cunt of yours?"

I groaned, gripping the counter harder. "I think if you keep talking dirty like that, I'm going to have to do something about it myself."

"Don't tease me. Keep your hands on the counter. Let me do my best work." And then his mouth was on me, spreading me as he slowly licked and explored me, his tongue a casual caress that was anything but casual. I groaned, trying to suck in a deep breath as he continued to explore me with his mouth and then his fingers. He stretched me, inserting one finger, and then another, and then a third somehow as he continued to suck on my clit, as if he had been doing this with me all our lives. I could barely suck in a breath, could barely breathe.

All that mattered was that he was on me, and I needed him. My toes curled inside my heels, my lower back tensed, and that warm sensation filled me, my breasts tightening, and as I tried to breathe, I came apart.

An unending orgasm shook through me and I might've screamed his name or said something, but I wasn't sure. All that mattered at that moment was that his mouth was on me, and I kept coming, the warm sensation of freedom and ecstasy all rolling into one.

Everett stood up and lifted me. He kept me steady

as he cupped my face and crushed his mouth to mine. "So fucking amazing."

I could taste myself on his tongue, and it just made me grind into him harder, needing him. My dress was still wrapped around my hips, and I knew I was wet, soaking his thigh as I rode him. I couldn't think, couldn't do anything. Then he had his hands up my dress, cupped my breasts over my bra, playing with my nipples. I ran my hands up and down his back, needing, exploring. And then he shoved me down, gentle and yet forceful. I gripped the edge of the sink as he pushed my dress more firmly over my curves, my ass in the air, as he palmed me, fingering me again as he molded my ass with one hand.

"I'm going to fuck you, Bethany. I'm going to fuck you so hard both of us will forget our names. What do you say to that, baby?"

"I say if you don't get inside me right now, show me how big that cock is, I'm never going to forgive you."

"That's my girl," he whispered before he sucked on my neck and began to fuck me harder with his fingers. The sound of wetness filled the kitchen, and I felt like I should've been embarrassed, but I wasn't. Instead, I rode his hand and came again, trying to catch my breath.

And then he was moving, the sound of his pants

unzipping filling my ears, the sweet eroticism making me yearn.

I heard the sound of the condom opening, sliding over his length, and then he was at my entrance, gently probing.

"Are you ready?"

"Everett."

He gripped my hip, squeezed, and wrapped my hair around his fist. "Say yes."

"Yes," I called out. Then he slammed into me, stretching me to the brink. Stars shattered beneath my eyelids as I tried to suck in a breath. He didn't even pause, continued to move, slamming into me once, twice, again and again as I moved back into him, pressing my ass into his hips, needing more, meeting him thrust for thrust.

It was raw, it was dangerous, it was everything that I had known I wanted.

This wasn't a casual awakening. This was every-thing. This was Everett and me.

This was him wanting me and seeing me as no one else had before.

I couldn't breathe, couldn't do anything other than move with him and want more. I was still mostly dressed, as was he, but it didn't matter.

"Bethany, I'm going to—" I nodded, his hand around

my throat, just slightly, keeping me steady as I arched, needing him closer. I didn't know how he could even be closer, but it's what I needed. And then he was coming, his lips on mine, as I came again, clamping down around him, shaking. I didn't know what happened next. I swore I blacked out.

But I found myself sitting on his lap, still feeling him pulsing inside me as he sat on a kitchen chair, his eyes wide, both of us disheveled.

"Well," he whispered. "Well."

I smiled at him, and then we both laughed, holding onto one another.

This was the Everett I had known before, but a different one. One with a little more danger, a little more sadness, but still with that twinkle in his eyes.

I liked this Everett. Even more than I had liked the one from our past.

And I knew that when we had to walk away, this was going to hurt. But I wasn't going to think about that. Instead, I just kissed him and slowly rocked over him as we smiled.

And I ignored the real world.

Because I had to.

# Chapter Ten

## Bethany

Everett kissed the small of my back, then sat up, rolling his shoulders. "I'm late for a Wilder family meeting. I need to get out of this bed, or I'm never going to leave."

I smiled over at him, content in my nakedness, just as he seemed to be.

"I have three calls today, a read-through, and travel planning. Plus, a workout before. So at some point, I'll see you again." I laughed as I said it, rolling over, loving the hunger in his eyes when I didn't bother to cover my breasts.

His gaze trailed down to the V between my legs and grinned.

"I hope I helped with the workout already."

I blushed, memories of how we'd worked out filling my mind. "Oh, I got my cardio in. I need to work on my strength training, however."

Everett frowned as he quickly got dressed. "I'm sure we can figure out something. Strength training and sex? I'm sure it's a thing."

"Oh, I bet you there are already porn tutorials on how to get a superhero body with just sex, but I don't think I have the energy for that. I might be too out of shape."

His eyes roamed over my body. "Oh, I like your shape. All curves and silk. I'm getting hard again."

I laughed. I couldn't help it. "How on earth are you already hard? You came as many times as I did."

"Well, that's a lie. You came way more times. Women are lucky with those multiple orgasms."

"We need something in our lives. Men get everything else."

"And on that note, I have a meeting, have fun today. I'll see you later." He pressed a kiss to my lips, then headed out. I watched his ass as he left. He had a great ass.

I knew I was playing with fire. That this wasn't

forever. I was supposed to have fun, to relax. And Everett was helping me do that. He did not want a future with me. Because having a future with me meant you had to go through the gauntlet of Hollywood and the press. Nobody wanted what came with an actor. I was still dealing with my previous relationship, even though I was glad that I was slowly fading from the headlines. People were still excited about my next movie, but now they were more focused on the family dynamics of a reality show kingdom that was beginning to fall. I honestly had no idea what was going on with them, but at least I was out of the headlines for now.

That would probably annoy Dallas.

I quickly headed back to the bathroom, piled my hair on the top of my head, and went to go work out.

I started with yoga to stretch, then I went through my strength training, grateful that my team had sent over weights and some other things for me. I could abuse the Wilder gym, but I didn't want anyone else to watch this. I had been very lucky that nobody had caught me on camera coming in and out of the facilities or around the property. In some aspects, I could understand feeling as if I were a prisoner here, but I didn't. I felt safe...which worried me.

It was going to be hard to say goodbye. I knew that. But this wasn't forever. This was just a blip in time, and then I would move on. And so would the Wilders. I pushed that depressing thought from my mind and went back to work, turning on my video chat with my trainer. If I was planning to be here any longer, they would probably come out in person, but for now, this was working.

I was getting a full sweat on when the doorbell rang. I sucked in a deep breath, losing my concentration.

"We are good for the day. You know what you need to do. Answer that. I will be back on tomorrow."

I breathlessly said thank you to my trainer as they logged off, and only slightly missed the sight of Malibu Beach behind them.

The Texas Hills were beautiful, especially where I was, so that was my view for now.

The doorbell rang again, like someone was leaning on it. I sighed, wiped the towel against my face, and grabbed my water bottle as I went to the door.

The Wilders had a cleaning service, but I hadn't had them come in because I wanted privacy. So I had done my own cleaning, and Everett had even helped me with the bathrooms. We had laughed over it as he had grumbled about that being part of his job. But he wanted me to be safe, so nobody else had been in this house except those I chose. I hadn't gotten a note from my stalker since that first one had shown up in my email, so I didn't expect it to be anything dangerous. Nobody knew where I was.

So when I opened the door, I blinked, confused.

"What the hell are you doing here?" I asked Dallas Huntington.

He smiled at me, his eyes contrite, his teeth bright white. His blond hair was pushed back from his face as if he had been running his hands through it, and Apollo himself had dusted his face with the perfect tan.

This was the man I thought I loved. The man that was fake behind the lines of whatever Hollywood pumped into his body. I thought he was the best I could do. I thought he loved me. So, I stayed with him.

Now all I saw in him were my own desires fading away and dying.

"Bethany, darling. You have no idea how hard it was to find you. We were looking for you everywhere."

That's when I realized he wasn't alone.

Cassandra Fox stood next to him, her plump mouth in a pout, her eyes wide. "I'm so sorry that we are just now finding you. We wanted to console you after everything that happened. But I know that is something that Dallas needs to go over. It would be better if the two of you were talking alone. But, since I'm with him now, the three of us need to formulate a plan of attack. Oh, Bethany. How these weeks must have been so hard on you. I can tell. I truly can. But we are here for you now. You don't have to hide your pain any longer. You can sleep. We will take care of it."

I had entered a level of hell, a new dimension with women who hated me, and nothing made sense.

I was friends with strong women. I was becoming friends with new women who were just as strong as Lark and me. And yet, the woman in front of me was weak. I knew that. She was weak because of how she treated me and others. I hated the culture that pitted women against each other, but Cassandra reveled in it.

Maybe in another world, we could have been friends. We could've ignored our adversaries, ignored the media, and found our own strength.

But that's not what Cassandra wanted. That's not what Ms. Fox wanted. And now, this was the world we lived in.

"Honestly, I have no idea why you guys are here or even how you got here. You are not welcome. We are not putting on a united front because you two are together now. Yes, you cheated on me, Dallas, but I don't care anymore. I honestly don't give a crap. Cassandra? You are welcome to him. Apparently, you were welcome to him when I thought he was still mine. I do not care. I do care about the fact that you keep trying to run this news cycle for your own careers. Get off this property, and don't come back."

Dallas moved forward, his eyes soft, pleading. But I saw a hint of anger in them. He did not like to be told what to do. No matter what he did, he was always in the right, even when he was screwing another woman in my office next to my awards.

"I'm just here to say I'm sorry."

I laughed, a full, deep-throated laugh that came straight from my stomach. "Don't even. You're never sorry about anything, Dallas. We both know that."

"Of course, I'm sorry. I'm sorry I hurt you and didn't leave you when I should have. Cassandra and me? We're the real deal. But our viewers? Our fans? They were hurt because of us. And that I cannot move on from."

"Us? No, *you* screwed her. You're the one who did this. They're hurt because of you."

Anger flashed in his eyes. "But they blame the both of us. They blame you, Bethany. And we need to show a united front as the three of us, so they know that we are in their corner. You know how fans get. You don't want them to go crazy."

I remembered that note that blamed me for leaving him. But he didn't know about that, so this couldn't be about that note. No, this was about him falling from the limelight.

"You need to go."

That's when he rubbed his nose again and began to scratch at his wrist. Just two slight tells, and my stomach rolled. He was high. I knew that he played around, that he tried things, and I had done my best to stop him. I thought he had quit. But from the way that Cassandra's pupils were dilated and how Dallas couldn't stand still, I thought they might both be high.

The studios weren't going to like that, and if this hit the news, it was just going to bring everything back up again. This wasn't good, and I wasn't sure how I was going to fix it, or even if I could. Or should.

But, damn it, I didn't want Dallas to hurt himself. I just wanted him to leave me alone.

"You need to go. Please. I'm not going to ask again."

"You never really understood us. What we could have become together. And the three of us? We could rule the world. And you are just going to be left behind. An old crone."

Cassandra laughed at Dallas's words, the two staring at each other with such adoration it made me ill.

I tried to catch up with my own thoughts and what the hell was going on. "How did you get through security?"

"I snuck in through security because I'm Cassandra Fox. Like you couldn't talk your way through anything. Oh, little girl, you aren't ready for what's coming next."

And, with that, she turned on her heel, Dallas following her like he was on a leash. My breath came out in angry pants, and I looked up to see Everett standing on the other side of the path. He stood to the side from where the happy couple walked, fists clenched. Rage covered his features, and I held out my hand, hoping that they didn't see him. That he wouldn't make a scene.

Because if he did, then this couple would use it. They would use anything that they could for their own gain.

I learned that far too late, and honestly, the hard way.

When they were out of earshot, Everett stormed up to me. "What the hell? Are you okay? How did they get here?"

I didn't realize my hands were shaking until I swallowed hard and hugged my sides.

"I don't know. You should talk with your security. I need to go back to work. I cannot allow their attitudes to affect what I do. I cannot allow anyone to affect my work and my life."

"Are you serious right now? What the hell did your ex just do? Did he hurt you?"

Everett reached out to me, but I took a step back, knowing that if he touched me, I would break. And I couldn't afford to break.

"What the hell, Bethany? Don't push me away. I'm not your ex."

"I know that. This isn't on you. Just go away, Everett. I need some space."

"No. You don't fucking get to do this. Don't push me away. Don't make me out to be the bad guy. I'm worried about you, Bethany. You're shutting down because of that fucker."

"I'm shutting down because I have work to do." I could hear my voice breaking, but I was a better actor than that. I needed to be. "Everett, I can handle this on my own."

"No, you damn well can't."

Then he stormed off toward Dallas, and panic seized me. I couldn't let him get in the middle of this. Dallas and Cassandra would do something to hurt him, and no matter what I felt, I couldn't let Everett get hurt because of me.

"If you confront him, it's over. If you make this worse than it already is, if you end up on the news because you beat up Dallas Huntington, I'll never speak to you again."

He whirled toward me, his eyes wide. "Why won't you let me stand up for you?"

We weren't attracting anybody's attention yet, but if he didn't leave the area soon, we would. I couldn't have this happen. Not to Everett. Not to the Wilders, when they had been so kind to me.

"If you make a scene, it will just make it worse. I can handle this on my own. I always have. I have a team in place for this, Everett. I need you to go back to your job to do what you do. Let me do mine."

"Because I'm just the soldier farm-boy here, and you're the princess in the tower? The celebrity I couldn't understand? Well, Bethany, as you fucking wish."

When he stormed off, tears threatened, but I could not cry. I could not do anything other than stand there, take a deep breath, and walk calmly back into my house. If I reacted in any way, if I slammed the door, if I screamed, others would hear, and it would reach the press. It would be all over social media. And it would just be worse than it already was. I needed to be calm and collected and hide behind my sunglasses and my own pride and pretend that I had it all handled.

My hand shook as I dialed Eli's number and let out a breath. "Eli? We have a problem."

I told him exactly what happened.

I knew that I needed to leave soon. That I overstayed my welcome with the Wilders.

And if I stayed any longer than I had, I would hurt Everett more.

And that was one thing I couldn't do.

# Chapter Eleven

Everett

I was beyond pissed off. Bethany had flipped me away as if I were an annoying fly and didn't have the right to want to take care of her or protect her. It was as if all of our time together had meant nothing, and I was indeed just that farm boy who didn't get the girl in the end.

I made my way to the main building, needing to yell at someone. Maybe Eli. Yes, he was a good target because he was supposed to be in charge of the security for the whole property. Yet Dallas and Cassandra had been able to enter the property with nobody knowing.

I wanted to know exactly how that had happened.

Before I could make it in, Elijah and Joy walked out, hand in hand. And from the scowl on Elijah's face and the way that he looked at me, I knew that word had spread.

"Come with me."

I scowled. "I'm sorry, you're not my dad. In fact, I'm older than you. Don't tell me what to do."

"Don't act like a jackass, and I won't have to tell you what to do."

"Always."

I looked over at Joy, but she shook her head at the both of us.

"Come with us. There are a few things we have to talk about, and it would probably be better if we didn't blast all of her news and life story to the guests here. Come on. We can handle this."

Joy sounded so calm and collected, and I didn't want to yell at her.

"Where am I supposed to go?"

"Follow me." Elijah sighed. "I'm trying not to order you around, but I'm asking. Eli is handling it. We will all handle it. But I know you, and if you are stomping over here already growling, then we have to have a talk."

I followed him, not because I wanted to, but because it was the right thing to do. And I trusted Elijah. It didn't matter that technically he was my little brother, he would always act like a big brother to all of us. Just like Eli.

It must be the suit. It was a perfect pair to Joy's business casual dress.

We made our way around the main building and towards East's hidey-hole. My twin had his own building for maintenance and other things, even though his main office was in the main house. I didn't see East around, so when Elijah gestured for Joy and me to go inside, I went.

"I don't think East is going to appreciate us being here."

"Probably not, but it was the closest place for privacy. This way you can yell, and nobody will hear you scream."

Joy rolled her eyes. "Oh, that's good. That's good. Make a horror movie where I'm alone in a place with sharp tools with two men."

I smiled, but it was only half-hearted. "You're safe with us." I paused. "So, I take it you know what happened with Bethany?"

"Part of it. Dallas Huntington and his new woman showed up and were able to get through security because she was on the guest list of the event."

I paused. "How the hell did that happen?"

"I'm not sure. Eli and Alexis are looking into it. But if you left Bethany alone in her cabin right now and are not going after that man, and something happened, I want to know."

I cursed under my breath. "She told me to go, so I did. I left her alone even though someone is sending her creepy emails. I left her alone because she said that she could handle everything and she didn't need me. I'm just the loser that was falling in love with her. She doesn't need me. She's a celebrity. A woman who's about to win a damn Oscar if the world has anything to say about it. And here I am, thinking I could be with her." I kept blurting out words, as if they would make sense. I hadn't meant to. I didn't even know they were on my mind until Elijah shook his head, and Joy gave me a pitying look.

"You don't have to handle everything for her. If Joy has taught me anything, it is that you don't just handle things for other people. Especially the woman that you're with. You have to find a compromise in which you find ways to be there for her. And help where she needs it. You don't take over. And you don't make a damn scene where you know that if the media caught wind of it they'd make an even bigger scene."

"He hassled her. I don't know what else happened

because she didn't tell me. But she's hurt. I don't want her to be hurt. She won't let me fix it."

"You can't fix everything," Elijah said solemnly.

"Elijah, you know my past. You know I couldn't fix it before. I couldn't. But I can fix *this*. I can help her. She just has to let me."

"You're not making any sense. How are you supposed to fix what happened over in the desert? You can't go back in time and make it better. You got hurt, and your other friends were lost. We all lost people over there. I know that thinking about it and trying to make it better doesn't work. You can't fix what pain you go through daily. But you could fix this. By apologizing."

I sputtered. "Apologizing? What for? She didn't even want me to stay to talk it out with her. She was so afraid I would make a scene with her pretty ex-boyfriend that she kicked me out."

"You're not making any sense. Do you want to make a scene? Do you want to stay and listen? How are you supposed to fix it if you don't talk with her?" Elijah began to pace.

"Because she wouldn't let me stay. How am I supposed to protect her if she won't let me stay?"

And that was the crux of it. Because she wasn't going to stay either, was she?

Joy bit her lip and stepped forward. "I know you can't protect her the way that you want to. Bethany is on a whole different level than all of us. Her career puts a different spin on what she needs. Which means she knows what she can handle. And you need to let her do that. You need to be with her and give her the time she needs, but if she saying that she knows how to handle a situation that you have never come across? You need to trust her. And if you don't? That's on your pride. Not hers."

I looked at the woman my brother had fallen in love with and sighed. "You're good for my brother, you know."

The two smiled at each other, seeming to have a thousand conversations in that one glance. "I know," they both said at the same time.

Damn it. I wanted that. I wanted that connection. That trust. The fact that it looked as if they could read each other's minds.

I might not have that with Bethany. Right now, we were just a fling while she hid from the real world. I didn't know what happened in her daily life, or how she handled being in the public eye. She was an oasis, and all I was, was a distraction.

I was a distraction.

I should've known. I *had* known. We were only

supposed to have until she went back to her real world, which was so far removed from the actual real world.

"What are you thinking?" Elijah asked.

"I think I need to learn how to grovel."

"I think he can help you with that. He's learned well." Joy winked.

That made me smile. "What tomfoolery has Elijah gotten into?"

My brother put his arm around Joy's shoulders and held her close. "We don't need to discuss that part. That is just for us."

"I'm going to mess this up. She's going to go. You know that, right? What we have? It's not real. It can't be. She's going to go away and do amazing things. Things I can't even begin to imagine. And I'm going to be left behind."

"Maybe not. It could work, you never know."

I wanted to believe Joy, only I didn't think I could.

I met my brother's gaze and saw the sadness there. "You have to decide what you want and what your worth is. If all you want is a moment with her, take it. If you think there could be more, try. But if you want more, and you know it's not going to happen, then you need to figure out what you want. But either way, you better grovel." He winked as he said it, and I tried to believe that I could do that. I could walk away if that was what was needed.

Only, I was not good at any of this. I never had been. My last serious relationship had been with Jennifer. And we hadn't even been serious. And now she was gone, and Bethany was going to leave.

Why did it feel like all I did was make mistake after mistake?

The door opened, and East walked in, a glare on his face. "Is there a reason that you're having a meeting in my office? Is there something that I missed? Are you trying to be like our in-laws and going in on a ménage of some sort? Of course, with siblings, I didn't think that was going to happen." He scowled as he said it, and Joy pushed at his shoulder, laughing.

"Sorry, East. You know the only Wilder I would let join our relationship is you. We already have it in the books."

East laughed from his chest, something I didn't often see from him, as he hugged Joy close. "I like this one, Elijah. Can we keep her?"

I fake glared between the two of them. "I'm really glad that I'm secure enough in our relationship that I know this is a joke. Because I do not want to have to bury my brother in the backyard."

"I don't know, I think East could take you." I ducked

Elijah's fist, even though he wasn't swinging too hard, and left, leaving the three of them with their own jokes.

East almost never smiled these days, so it was nice to see him laugh. Joy brought that out in him. She was just kind, she was good for Elijah for sure. But it seemed that she might be good for the family as well.

Elijah had found someone, same with Evan and Eli and Eliza. And yet, what about me?

Why did I keep falling for the one person I couldn't have?

I made my way down the path towards the gray cabin, knowing I needed to talk with Bethany. When the cabin came into view, I stiffened, seeing Eli and two of our security team leaving Bethany alone. Eli met my gaze, nodded at her, and then left, everybody going over plans of some sort on a tablet.

I looked at Bethany, looking so small on the porch, and all I wanted to do was wrap her up in my arms and never let go.

But I knew she wouldn't let me do that.

And even if she did, it wouldn't be for long.

She finally looked over at me, and I stared, not knowing what to say. I should've come up with a plan, a script. Something that would make sense, and yet all I could do was look at her and want to take away her pain. But that had never been my job when it came to her. Had never been my role. But I wanted it to be. I wanted to fix it all. But I couldn't. No matter what. I couldn't.

"Did my brother and the team take care of you?" I asked, my voice rough.

She looked at me, a small smile on her face. "They did. I have my own security coming out as well. They apparently should've been here the whole time, but I was so set on doing things on my own that I ignored my rules. I have to stop ignoring my own rules."

She met my gaze as she said it, and it was a dagger to my heart. Yet, at the same time, I knew she was afraid. Afraid of that note, afraid of her ex and what he could do. This wasn't about me, and I needed to remember that.

I didn't get to be angry because she wasn't relying on me in a way that a long-term relationship would. We were a fling, something we had both known when we had gone into this.

It didn't matter that we had a past of a few nights. Those days were long over, and we both had emotional baggage that could fill an airplane. I would just have to remember where we were and what we were.

And I couldn't take out my frustrations on her.

"I'm sorry. For walking away. For yelling. For being an asshole. You don't deserve that. I'm sorry." I stuck my hands in my pockets, and she stared up at me, her eyes wide.

"I'm sorry for pushing you away. I need to handle these things on my own, too, Everett. I've been doing it for a while now, and I was listening to my own instincts before. And that's why I got so angry and pushed you. But I can't have anyone else control these things for me. I have to be able to do them on my own even if it doesn't make sense."

"I just wish I could fix it all for you with the snap of my fingers. To look at a spreadsheet and some numbers and make it work. But that's not how it is, and I have to remember that."

"We're both very good about talking around the issues." She looked up at me. "I have work. I have to travel for work and do countless interviews, even more than I've been doing from the comfort of this cabin. Everything is a whirlwind outside of this moment with you, and that means everything is going to change soon. I don't know how I'm going to be able to say goodbye when it's time. I just want you to know that. I'm not good at this. But I'm trying."

It was as if she were twisting the knife harder, but it had nothing to do with her. Now it was my own feelings. I knew where this would end, and it wasn't going to be pretty, but I just had to think of this moment. She wasn't pushing me away this time, so I leaned forward and brushed my lips against hers.

"Invite me inside, Bethany."

She smiled against my lips and then sat up, tugging at my shirt. "Is this your way of apologizing? Because I have a way to say I'm sorry as well."

I chuckled, pushing all thoughts of what could hurt us away, knowing it wouldn't help. I needed to focus on her, only on her.

She led me into the cabin and I locked the door behind us.

I ran my hands over her hair, kissing her gently as we stood in the small dining room, slowly exploring one another, no words needed. Because words would just break us in the end. Truths and tribulations and everything that had to do with reality would cut jagged shards within our souls.

We just had to live in the moment.

But maybe I was in love with the Bethany that was here, not the one that would soon have to go back to work and be the face of so many talents. There would be no place for me there, just like I knew I couldn't hide her away from the world here.

We could have this instant. And I could have this taste.

So I kissed her harder, slowly running my hands

over her body. She led me to the bedroom, and I was grateful. My dick hardened, pressing against the seam of my jeans. I licked my lips, then kissed her again, slowly stripping her from her clothes. I wanted her bare before me, in more ways than one. But I would take what I could get. Even if it broke me in the end.

She stripped me as well, and then we were both on the bed, my mouth rolling over her body, over her breasts. I licked and sucked at her nipples, languidly feasting on her flesh. She was warm and sweet, and all I wanted to do was press against her and take her as mine. We rolled so I was on my back, and she grinned down at me as she slid down my body.

"What are you doing?" I whispered.

"What I want. For once."

I sighed before I groaned, watching the way her head bobbed between my legs, her mouth warm and hot around my length. She continued to suck, cupping my balls as she did. She hollowed her mouth, working me as if she knew every inch of me. As if she knew what got me going, and damn straight she did. I ran my hands through her hair, over her shoulders, anything I could reach. And when my balls tightened and I nearly came, I pulled her away and flung her down on the bed, twisting so I hovered between her legs.

"How did you move that quickly?"

I winked, sliding my thumb along her clit. "I'm practicing with you. How am I doing?" But before she could answer, I had my mouth on her pussy, her body arching to meet me. We were at the edge of the bed, so she propped herself up on her elbows so I could reach her breasts, playing with her nipples as I continued to eat her out. She tasted like peaches—sweet, tart, tempting. And all mine.

She continued to writhe against my face, wet, sloppy, and everything I wanted. I could feast on her until the end of my days, diving between her legs like a man dying of hunger and thirst. If this was all I could eat for the rest of my life, I would be damned happy.

So when she came, my chin dripping with her juices, I grinned, then licked up her body, and captured her mouth with mine.

It was the hottest thing I'd ever done, watching the way she writhed against me, wrapping her thighs around me, my dick pressed against her wetness. I held back a curse and then reached into the bedside table, where I knew she kept condoms. She took the packet from me, opened it quickly, and then slid it down my length in the most erotic vision I had ever seen.

And then I was on my back, her hovering above me.

Her long hair traveled down her chest, covering her

breasts. She looked like a siren, singing me to my doom. And I would follow wherever she was leading.

I held her hips, and then she slowly, oh so slowly, slipped down on me. Her cunt pulsed around me, tightening with every slight rotation of her hips. I had to grit my teeth to not come right then and there.

And then she began to move.

Slow strokes with just a slight undulation of her hips. I couldn't breathe, couldn't think. I let my body do the motions, both of us moving as one. I cupped her breasts then moved to pull her down to me, needing her mouth. I held her close, one hand between us to play with her, the other hand on her hip, keeping her steady as I pounded into her from below. I breached her other entrance, both of us groaning as I used her wetness to make it easier.

I was fucking her with my cock and my finger at once, both of us groaning at the sensations.

When she came, she moaned my name. I continued to move, the vibrations of her orgasm sending me over the edge. When it was over, I held her close, needing her, and knowing that this moment was in a snow globe. A piece of memory and time forever encased in nothingness.

Because the glass would shatter soon, the real world would invade.

But, until then, I had Bethany.

I had her.

And when she fell asleep in my arms later, I stayed awake, knowing it would give me a headache. But it didn't matter.

She had been scared, and changes were coming. But, for now, we could pretend.

Pretend we had a future.

Pretend she would want a Wilder.

# Chapter Twelve

Bethany

My feet pounded down the path, sweat sliding down my chest, down my back. Everything ached, probably because I had gone eight miles instead of five. But it had been such a wonderful day, and I hadn't been able to sleep. I had watched the sun rise over the hills as I ran, and now we were going back to work, doing research for my next part, and going over my script. I had a lot to do. I felt like I was behind, even though this was a scheduled break from my real life.

Of course, reality stalked me in the form of my

bodyguard, a few feet behind me, jogging as if Trace were enjoying himself.

I knew Trace could out-run me, out-lift me, and pretty much out-everything me, but he had the grace to pretend that he was finished with his jog as well.

Of course, he wasn't panting at all, while I had a stitch in my side, and I felt like heavy breathing wasn't going to help.

"I hate you sometimes," I growled as Trace chuckled.

He checked the security system on the little gray cabin and then walked me inside as I went to get us water and protein shakes.

Trace had worked with me since soon after I had met Everett, oddly enough. I had gotten my dream job, and my rise in stardom—as the tabloids had put it—had increased in popularity, and I'd needed help when I was out of my house. I hated this part of the job, but at least Trace and his team were nice. I'd forced them not to come with me for my vacation because I thought it would be safe, and so far, I had been—physically. Emotionally, digitally, and dealing with my ex, not so much. But now he was here, and it was just one more thing that I had to deal with.

"You only hate me because you run whole-hearted as if I don't have a mile of leg on you. It takes you two steps for every one of mine. I know you try to keep pace with me."

I rolled my eyes and tossed him his water bottle as I guzzled mine down. I swallowed and wiped my brow. "Excuse me, but you don't point out the fact that I'm struggling to keep up with you."

"You're the one who wanted to do eight miles after a full-strength workout. But you do you. Now, how about I work on the protein shakes, and you go get ready for your day?"

I winced. "I have a lot to do when I'm just sitting at my desk. Are you sure that you want to sit here and watch?"

Trace rolled his eyes. "You know that's not what I do. Even though it sounds like exactly what I do, and I'll have to be in the house with you for the rest of the day. Not that I don't adore you." He winked as he said it, which made me laugh.

"Sorry, where are you going to be? Hidden in the bushes somewhere in case my ex comes back?"

A dark shadow passed over his gaze, and I was annoyed that I had even said anything about it.

"He shouldn't have gotten on the property, and the Wilders know it."

"It wasn't their fault."

"We are not talking about whose fault it was. We

should have been here. I shouldn't have listened to you. Even though you are my boss."

"I thought we had a partnership going on." I winced, and he shook his head.

"Whatever, Bethany. I need to keep you safe. And I know that man of yours wants to keep you safe, too."

I blushed. "Everett is a friend."

"We don't lie to each other. That was the rule. However, I'm not going to pry. That's not my job."

"You sure are a little wishy-washy with the parameters of your job," I said dryly.

"It's amazing what happens when you can actually speak to one another about crap like that." He let out a breath and handed me my protein shake. "Drink this, then another bottle of water, and get your work done. I'm working with Wilders' security, and we've got you covered. Frank will be with you anytime you leave the property. Though I realize that's actually not all that often."

I shrugged, feeling a little hemmed in. "I'm going to be all over the world soon, with press junkets and shooting on location. Not going to have time to just sit down. I could've done this in LA, but they are right outside the gates. At least for now, I'm sort of hidden." I paused. "Except that Dallas found me."

"Dallas found you because of the leak, and we

plugged it. You're keeping on the down-low here, and you're doing the best you can. We've got you, Bethany. We're going to keep you safe."

Someone knocked on the door, and Trace looked at his phone, nodded, then gestured towards it. "It's your man. Glad I put that camera out there, but I think you need to put more motion sensors in."

"This isn't our place, Trace. We don't need to put barbed wire around it. I'm trying to blend in, remember?"

Trace began to grumble some more, and I snorted before I went to the door and opened it. Everett stood there, three cups of coffee on a tray in his hands, and a smile on his face. "I have work to do, and so do you, before dinner with the Wilders tonight. However, I wanted to see if you needed coffee, and to get a kiss since I had to leave you for a meeting early this morning."

I blushed, thinking about why I had been able to sleep the night before and how early he had left. Of course, I was also nervous as hell because I had dinner with his entire family tonight.

That seemed like a very big step, especially because we were both purposely not talking about our relationship. Because we couldn't talk about our relationship. There couldn't be one, not with me leaving so soon. And not with the fact that he wouldn't want anything to do with the reality of my life.

He pressed his lips to mine, and I swallowed hard, trying not to think about the fact that my time was running out.

"Thank you for the coffee. I take it one is for Trace?"

"Of course. The guy who's protecting you needs to be able to have his wits about him. And I know how he needs his caffeine intake."

"Good man, Wilder. I'm headed out to do another perimeter check, and then she's on her own for a bit, even though we're around. So take your time." Trace saluted me as he nodded at Everett, took his coffee, and headed out.

I laughed, shaking my head. "He's not very subtle."

"I like him. I mean, I didn't think I would like a guy who is constantly around you, but he's protecting you. I like him."

I reached up and pushed his hair from his forehead. "He's a good man. His whole team is great. And I didn't have them here because I didn't want to be *the* Bethany Cole when I was here. Now it seems like I don't have a choice."

"He'll keep Dallas and whoever else is with him off our property. Just like our team will. You're safe here, Bethany."

"Nothing is dangerous, though. It's just that stupid asshole. I just hate the fact that I even have to have security. It's part of my payroll system and everything. I hate to think about it every budget that I do, even with what I make."

I winced. I tried not to talk about money with him because we were in far different circumstances. But I had only recently come into the earnings I was making. And I knew with the snap of a finger, things could completely change, and I could end up broke. So I invested, and I tried not to spend my money unwisely. So having to shell out for a security team grated on me. Even if I liked Trace and the rest of them.

Storms clouded over Everett's face, and he gave me a tight nod before he kissed me soundly. "I have to head to work. But the whole point of them being here is so that way anything violent doesn't happen to you. It's better to be safe than sorry."

I heard the worry in his tone, and I understood it. It was such an odd thing to actually have to use body-guards. But I wasn't the only one in my profession to use or need them.

Finally, he kissed me again, then headed to the main building to work, while I went to shower and actually get ready for my day. While I would be alone in the house for a while, I knew that my security team was still around in case I needed them. I was never truly alone, and that frustrated me more than I could say.

Maybe it was just that I was weary.

I went through my notes, did some stretching, and began working on my script. I only had a couple of weeks left until I had to go back to the real world. And once I did, I would have to once again be the actress that I was. That meant knowing my lines.

I rolled my shoulders back, went through what I needed, and texted Lark back, hoping she was sleeping by now.

I sighed and opened up my email, knowing that even though a few hours had passed, I still didn't have enough time to get through them all before I needed to get ready for my dinner.

I scrolled through the urgent ones and answered back what I could, but my team had done a good job of making sure that all pertinent emails went to them as well, so they handled it.

It was when I saw the subject line of one that my body turned to ice.

**Subject: it's time. don't you think?**

*Oh Bethany,*

*You tried. You really did. But you hurt us. Can't you*

*see what you're doing? You keep hiding, but he found you. So will I.*

*He loves you. And you hurt him. You hurt us.*

*I'll never let this happen again. I'll never let the darkness invade our lives. So I will do what I can to protect us. Whatever I can, Bethany Cole.*

*You hurt him.*

*Two will not hurt me again.*

*See you soon.*

Bile rose in my throat and I swallowed hard before I forwarded the email to my team and Trace. Trace was inside my house before I could blink, and he took my computer from me, talking into his phone. He kept grumbling as Frank, another member of the team, walked through my house as if they were afraid the sender of the email would be in my bedroom, hiding behind the closet door. The fact that that thought sent shivers down my spine told me I was already on edge.

"Are you okay?" Trace asked, closing my computer and taking it with him.

"I'm fine. It's just an email. You can't have my computer, I need it for work."

"You can have your computer back after I do a few more checks. I want to make sure that there is no way that they can find where you are. And, frankly, you don't need to be reading your email right now."

"I don't appreciate you telling me what to do," I said, rage and worry entwined within me.

"It's my job right now. Go get ready for your date with the Wilders. We'll go through what we can to ensure that this email is just a joke. But it doesn't sound like one."

I nodded tightly, my hands fisted at my sides. "No. It sounded different, didn't it? I don't know why they think that they were in a relationship with me and Dallas. It's like they don't believe anything other than the fact that it's my fault. And that they'll see me soon? I don't like that."

"I don't like the fact that you are about to leave this property to go to Eli Wilder's house."

"I'll be safe there. I have to be. I can't let this email chain me to a little cabin on the resort. Just like I couldn't let it keep me in my house in LA."

Trace studied my face, his jaw tightening. "You need freedom, but you also need to be safe. We're going to go talk with Eli and keep him in the loop. Especially because we'll be at his house tonight. With his family."

Chills shot through me. "They wouldn't hurt them, would they? It's just emails. They haven't really threatened me."

"I don't want them to threaten you beyond what they're doing, or even continue doing what they're doing now. But it is my job to think carefully. To be two steps ahead." He paused. "I know it's none of my business, but if you're going to go tonight, you should tell Everett. Eli will know, so Everett will want to hear from you personally."

I shook my head. "You need to stay out of my relationship, Trace."

He held up a hand. "Whatever you say, Ms. Cole."

I scowled at his tone, then let him walk away with my computer. I would get it back because they weren't going to find anything. There was nothing to find.

But I hated the fact that Trace was right. So, I picked up my phone, headed to my bedroom, and closed the door, dialing Everett's number.

"Hey there, Bethany. I was just thinking about you. I know you're busy all day until I pick you up for dinner, but what do you say to a cupcake from the kitchen?"

I was glad that I hadn't video called him. Because my heart hurt, and tears burned my eyes. "Everett, I need to tell you about an email. I don't want you to get angry. Or worried. Or all alpha male."

He was silent for so long that I feared I had made a mistake. I should've just kept it to myself, except for the fact that Eli was going to know. Therefore Everett needed to. And Trace was right. I had to be the one to tell him.

"Are you okay?"

"I'm fine." I told him about the email, exactly what it said, and what Trace and the team were doing.

Again, he was silent, until he finally sighed. "I want to say many things, but none of it is productive because it's not your fault. I'm glad that you told me and that the team is working on it. But if I hold your hand a little bit harder than necessary in the car to Eli's, let me?"

I smiled softly. "Okay. I can do that." I let out another breath. "I need to go. I'll see you soon?"

"With cupcakes," he promised.

He hung up, and I stared my phone, wondering how we would walk away, because I would need to.

Sooner than I wanted.

"Wait, why were his pants down?" I asked, as Joy threw her head back and laughed and Kendall clapped her hands.

"He said it was because he thought a scorpion had jumped up the leg of his pants, but I think he just wanted to show me his dick." Kendall fluttered her eyelashes and set her hands on her rounded belly. I wanted to reach out and feel the babies kick, but I didn't know her that well. At Kendall's warm smile, she reached for my hand and set my palm right above the curve.

"They're sleeping right now, but you might get a little kick."

My eyes widened as what felt like a little foot slamming into my palm sent shockwaves through me.

"Wow. They're strong."

Kendall winced. "They're strong when they are playing soccer on my bladder. But right now, I think that was just a little kick to say hello."

"I can't believe there are two of them in there right now."

"Me either. I don't feel like there's enough space, and yet I feel like a whale."

"If you call yourself a whale one more time, I'm going to spank you," Evan Wilder called out from the kitchen.

"If you keep threatening to spank me, I'm going to let it happen. And watch that sauce. The only reason I let you kick me out of the kitchen is that you said you wanted me to entertain Bethany. So here I am." She threw her hands in the air, scowling at her husband.

I looked over at Joy, and we both burst out laughing.

"I see marriage has taken with the both of you," Joy put in, her lips pursed.

"Oh, I'm just a bundle of marital joy," Kendall said dryly. "The closer I get to their due date, the more over-protective he gets. He's like a bear with a thorn in his paw."

"I think it's sweet. Even though I could never get through the day with all the growling," I teased.

"You're with Everett. He's the sweet one. Well, him and Elliot," Joy put in, sipping her wine.

"So, Elijah isn't sweet?" Alexis asked as she walked towards us, grinning. "Because if not, I'm going to need details."

I met Kendall's gaze, then we both grinned at the other woman.

"Really. I'm going to need all the details," I added.

Joy blushed. "Oh. Well. You know. I kind of like the growling."

I burst out laughing, the other girls joining in, as we talked about our men.

I knew this was a mistake. Because I kept calling them *our* men. Like Everett was mine. Like we had a future. I wanted to at least try, even if only for a moment.

I knew I was waiting for the other shoe to drop, and our time was limited. But sitting around with the

Wilders, with these women, it felt like a weird and real family.

A part of me, a very small part of me, wanted this to work.

But I knew it couldn't.

Because no matter what, this wasn't my future.

Everett didn't want my life outside of this bubble of normality. And as soon as the press caught wind of us, they would ruin that sense of peace that we had.

And I refused to do that to him.

A strong arm slid around my waist, and I turned to see Everett. He leaned forward, kissed my forehead, and scowled at Kendall. "Shouldn't you be sitting down? Evan, shouldn't your wife be sitting down?" he called out.

"Narc!" Kendall spat, but she sat down quickly, Joy turning so she blocked Evan's view.

Evan stormed out, his eyes narrowed as he looked at his wife. "What did I say about your ankles?"

"You said I was a fat cow and that my ankles were too swollen for me to be standing."

Everett sucked in a breath through his teeth, and I slowly stepped back with him, the girls doing the same.

"I did not say that. I said that your ankles were swelling because the doctor said you were on your feet too much. You are pregnant with twins. Why are you making me out to be the growly man?"

"Because you did this to her," Joy put in, and then put her hand over her mouth, as if she were startled she'd said the words.

Elijah, who had come to stand beside her, began to laugh.

"That's why I love you. Always sticking up for the girls and putting down my brothers. It's perfect."

My heart swelled at the look on Joy's face when Elijah said that he loved her. I knew that he did, but him saying it so freely? It was wonderful. All of the Wilders did that.

Not that Everett and I said that to each other. Because we didn't. We were just casual. Here I was, at a family dinner, and everyone was treating me like this was normal. That I was family.

I needed to walk away.

"Well, if it's my fault that you're in this position, I guess you're going to have to listen to me from now on," Evan said with a laugh.

"I don't think that's how that works," Kendall warned, and the two were at it again. Play fighting as a form of foreplay.

I smiled softly, even though my stomach still hurt,

thinking about the fact that this was only temporary for me.

Thankfully, Everett didn't seem to notice my distractions, and soon we sat down to eat, East being our chef for the night, and I ate almost nothing because I couldn't focus.

Again, I didn't think anyone noticed, as everyone was so focused on everything else with the babies coming, the new house preparations, and Wilder business.

But my mind was on a thousand different things.

When it was time to leave, Everett drove me home, and I smiled softly, yawning as I walked towards my front door.

"Are you going to tell me what's wrong?" he asked.

"I'm just tired. I had a long day."

He met my gaze and nodded. "I know you have. Thank you for coming, and I know you might've wanted to stay here with that email and everything, but I appreciate you coming out with my family. They like you, Bethany. I like you."

I smiled, even though I know it didn't reach my eyes, because everything was hurting.

Because this couldn't be my future. This was only supposed to be a fling.

Walking away was going to hurt, hurt far more than anything ever had in my life.

I had let him walk away before, because we hadn't had a choice. And now we were both in very different situations, and there was no changing that.

So, I had to be the one to go. To make the cut clean and more manageable.

"Everett," I began, and his face closed off.

He knew. Of course, he did.

"Bethany," he whispered.

"Bethany?" Trace asked from the darkness as he came forward, phone in his hand and scowl on his face.

I pulled myself out of my reverie as Everett turned to look at him, and I knew something was wrong from the stern expression on Trace's face and the scowl firmly in place. I swallowed hard.

"What is it?

"The press knows you're here, and they are at the gates. It's going to be a wild night."

And just like that, it was over.

# Chapter Thirteen

Everett

"Is it true that Bethany Cole is here?"

"Is it true that Bethany Cole is hiding after a disastrous facelift nightmare?"

"Is Bethany here with her secret lover she was caught cheating with on poor trusting Dallas Huntington?"

"Is Ms. Cole here preparing for an underdog cowboy hick romance movie?"

"Is Bethany Cole so sure she's going to lose that Oscar that she's already in mourning and in hiding?"

"Has Bethany Cole gone into hiding because she can't take the truth?"

. . .

I ignored the shouting from people with cameras as I pulled onto the property, knowing that legally there was nothing I could do because they were on public land. It would become my problem as soon as they touched Wilder land, but the authorities here weren't quite sure what to do with the paparazzi.

It wasn't like this area north of San Antonio, Texas, ever really dealt with them.

Perhaps George Strait might've owned a home near here, and ZZ Top at one point played at a bar often in another town near here, but that was as famous as this area got. At least as far as the authorities knew.

I had left Bethany alone after she finally fell asleep, her team and security going over plans for extraction.

Extraction.

That was the word they used for getting her out of Texas, away from prying eyes. Because they needed to *extract* her from the life she was currently living, so she could get back to a normal one that she could handle.

My head began to throb, nausea hitting, and I slowly pulled off to the side of the road, letting Eli pass me. He pulled off in front of me and got out of the car as I gripped the steering wheel and counted to ten. I needed to let the nausea pass, so I could breathe and get over today.

I needed to find a way to calm Bethany down so she could think clearly. So she would know that she wasn't alone and that we would be there for her. That *I* would be there for her.

I couldn't let her leave.

"Open up, Everett."

I opened the window and Eli reached in and squeezed my shoulder. "Do you need me to drive?"

I shook my head, then pressed my fingers to my temples, the pounding intensifying.

Eli cursed under his breath as I noticed Alexis get out of the passenger seat and get into the driver's seat of their car. I cursed under my breath, then got out of my truck, going around the front so I could get in the passenger side.

"Thanks for driving. I shouldn't have left this morning, but I had physical therapy."

"Bethany wanted you to go, and so did we. I'm just sorry that I didn't drive you as I should have. Things have been a little insane right now."

I looked over at him and frowned. "You could say that again." I looked out the window at the rolling hills as we made our way to the main house. Nothing seemed right, as if this wasn't the place where I had finally found my home.

After spending years moving around the world, no longer near my brothers, only able to see them in fractions of stolen moments, it felt like the six of us were finally home. The only way it would've been perfect was if Eliza would've been able to move with us.

But she had married into a large family that loved her, and had opened their arms to us as well. So, we had connections to Colorado through her, and we saw her as much as possible.

But the six of us Wilder brothers, thrown across the world and jagged around the edges, were finally coming together in this awkward puzzle that didn't really fit but was still finding a way.

This retreat, this winery, and everything that came with it, even the hassles and heartaches, had pulled us closer together than ever.

And yet it didn't feel real. At least not right now. It felt like I was making mistake after mistake because I wanted something that wasn't there. I wanted something that couldn't be mine.

I was just so tired. Tired of my head always hurting. Tired of guilt. Tired of memories.

Tired of knowing that Bethany was going to leave.

Just like she'd always promised.

This was the path that we had been led to, there was no going back.

And I didn't know how to fight for her without fighting with her. And she had enough on her plate for me to do the latter.

"You should go see her. You left for medical reasons, and she knows that. So go see her. We've got all of this."

"You have people hounding the front gates, and we have events today. I'm not quite sure that that's what you want."

"I know you aren't blaming Bethany for this, Everett."

I turned toward Eli. "Of course, I'm not. I'm blaming that fucking asshole. You know Dallas did this."

It was too much of a coincidence for it not to be him. He got even after not getting what he wanted, though I still didn't know what that had been. So he lashed out.

"It seems the most likely, but the thing is, Bethany Cole is a household name. She could wear as many ball caps and sunglasses as she wants, but somebody was bound to notice her. And yes, we value the privacy of our guests, but we can't prohibit phones. But you're right, it was probably Dallas trying to keep his name in the limelight or whatever he wants. Bethany deserved some peace and quiet, and she got some. But I don't know if we're the best place for her right now."

I whirled on him. "You want her to leave?"

Eli gave me a pitiful look, and I hated to see it on his face. "I don't want either of you unhappy. But I have to think of the safety of Bethany *and* our guests. She'll make her decision, and we will stand by it. I will not kick her out. But you have to face the reality, Everett. Things are going to change. They already have. I want to be ready for that."

I loved my own brother with everything that I had, but in that moment I hated him. I got out of the truck, slammed the door behind me, and stomped towards my office.

"I take it you don't want the keys then," Eli called out, and I flipped him off, storming inside past Naomi and Amos, who were getting ready for the day. They had their heads bent close to one another, whispering, and I kept going, ignoring the jealousy I felt at that.

Because they could be in the open like this, flirting their way through the initial phases of whatever relationship they had, and I had to hide everything with Bethany.

"Good, you're here," East said as he leaned against the door of my office.

"Is there something that you need?"

My twin glared at me, then shook his head. "I wanted to see how you were doing, ass munch. I know you had PT this morning, and it probably wasn't fun. I usually get a damn headache afterward, so I was checking up on you. I'm sorry I couldn't be there to drive you home. It was a miscommunication on my part."

"You don't need to take care of me. Not everybody in this damn family needs to take care of me."

East shook his head. "We all take care of each other. You guys baby me to no end because you're all afraid I'm going to suddenly break from not telling you my damn feelings every day. That is what we do. So, get over yourself and go see your woman."

"Why are you mad at me?" I shouted.

"Because you're yelling at me because you're in a bad mood. I'm sorry, I just wanted to make sure you're okay. I love you, you asshole. You're my twin. We're closer than any of the other siblings. Because we shared a gestation pod for a while."

"Is that what you're calling a womb?" I asked, trying to hold back laughter.

"I didn't want to scream the word 'womb' in a hallway when I know guests could be walking by."

I pressed my lips together, grateful for the levity. "So you screamed gestation pod?"

"Now I'm the one with the headache. Go see your woman."

"She doesn't want to see me."

"Then see why."

"I can handle this on my own, East."

"You're not handling it right now."

"By the way," East called out. I turned and looked at him over my shoulder. "Joy is over at her place now, packing. So I would get over whatever is wrong with you right now and talk with her. Because you're not going to have a chance to fix this before it's too late."

And at that, my twin left me standing alone in a hallway, wondering what the hell I was doing.

I slammed my way into my office, closing the door behind me, and let out a breath. Yes, my head ached, but it had nothing to do with PT, or my TBI. No, it had everything to do with the fact that I was once again leaving Bethany alone. She had asked because, apparently, she could handle this on her own. And I couldn't.

She was leaving. Why wouldn't she?

After everything that the press was screaming at our cars, why would she want to stay? There was no need for her to. Not with everything coming at her.

The press screamed accusations and speculation on why she was here. If they knew she was with me—what would they say then?

I shifted uncomfortably as I sat down on the chair, frowning. I didn't want to be in the press with her. I didn't want the world to know my name. I didn't want to be famous. I just wanted Bethany.

But the problem was that they were a package deal.

Would the press find out how I had been hurt? What I had done overseas? It might've been under orders. I might've been doing what my country told me to. But I had seen death, war, pain, and loss. I stood in the desert as the sun hit my face, wondering how I was ever supposed to live at home again when nothing else felt the same.

I was finally coming to terms with what it meant to be with my family again, and I didn't want the world to know that.

I might have told Bethany everything that happened, how I felt, and the friends that I lost, but that didn't mean I'd stop blaming myself for surviving.

They might call it survivor's guilt, but the guilt didn't go away. It scraped at your soul until there was nothing left. It haunted your dreams.

I still had the dreams when Jennifer, Clayton, Jericho, and Todd would stand around my office, or in the fields, and watch me.

I would see them in my dreams when I was grocery shopping. Doing mundane things. And they would stand there as if they had been there all this time.

They would shout at me, give me looks.

"Why did you forget me? I've been here all this time. Why are you letting me go? I never died. I never left you. Why did you move on?"

And I would run because I was too afraid to think that was the truth. In the dreams, it would be like they were really there, screaming at me and pulling at me, telling me that I had given up on them. That I had left them behind. That I moved on with my life and I hadn't mourned enough.

And then I would wake up in a sweat and think for an instant it was true. That they would call me any minute and tell me that they were still here. That I had moved on and forgotten and that there was no turning back.

That was the guilt that I held.

It wasn't for surviving.

The guilt came from living.

I pressed my fingers against my temple and told myself I needed to stop doing this. No therapy, no speaking, no connections with the family that I had would change this. The guilt would always be there.

But Bethany was here, too. At least for now.

And I couldn't protect my friends. I didn't think I could protect Bethany the way that she needed.

But I loved her.

And I needed to not be a damn coward anymore and tell her.

Only, I didn't know what would happen when I did. Or who I would be when she left.

Because the thing was, not even my dreams of the past that lured me back into a sense of security were truly what stood in my way.

No, it was the fact that Bethany had to leave.

And I would have to let her.

Because I loved her and I couldn't hold her back. But, maybe, there would be another way.

I just had to think of it first.

# Chapter Fourteen

Bethany

Somehow, over a month's worth of packing was done in only an hour. Though I hadn't brought much and only bought a few things. I had treated this as a camping trip, not entirely living out of my suitcase, but close enough. As if I had been prepared to move at a moment's notice, to leave when things got too difficult. When I needed to keep others safe.

Now was that time.

I had wanted to leave the night before to save the Wilders this embarrassment and pain of having to deal with me.

I wasn't the one standing outside the gates, demanding to be let in to hound the staff and anyone who might've seen me. But I had been the one to bring them here. With my mere presence, I had changed the dynamics of the Wilders.

I didn't just mean the property or company that had welcomed me with open arms. The family had done much the same, and I was causing a headache just by existing. I needed to leave.

Joy had left quickly after packing up some of my final items. She'd helped search the house to make sure I hadn't forgotten anything. While I knew it was because she wanted to help keep me occupied, part of me resented that I wouldn't be leaving a part of myself behind, that it was so easy to be erased. There wouldn't be a memory of me here other than what was etched on their minds.

Everything would be gone, and there would be no proof of me being here because the paparazzi had finally found me.

Then they would leave. They would follow me to the ends of the earth trying to get their story, because I had still not commented on my relationship with Dallas Huntington.

I had not explained that he had cheated, had tried to break my heart, tried to ruin me.

Instead, I said I wanted privacy through my publicist, and I had left. They had seen that act alone as a reaction, a retreat. Me running away with my tail tucked between my legs as I tried to hide.

It didn't matter that some were doing the math on how quickly Dallas and Cassandra seemed to be finding their forever romance. It didn't matter that the whispers of infidelity were already out there.

Dallas was perfection, and I had been on top too long. It was time for me to topple, prove to the world that everything wasn't as perfect as they said.

They had called me the girl who wasn't like other girls, a title I had rejected and despised. Because what was so wrong with being like other girls? What was so wrong with having common interests with your friends and girls that you looked up to? Girls that looked up to you?

There was nothing wrong with being like other girls, and that was one title I squashed quickly.

Then I had been the current "It" girl, and they waited for me to party too hard, to fall on my face. To say something stupid in an interview. They'd asked me questions on foreign policy and our country's politics. They had tried to trip me up with every single word I said, but had laughed with Dallas as if he were one of the good ol' boys.

Nothing had changed in the years since the golden era of movies. Fred Astaire could dance, sing, and act, while Ginger Rogers had to dance just like he did, but in heels and backward. That was the refrain people used to say—that women had power and were amazing and women could do anything. And then they would keep moving, and no one remembered that Ginger never got paid the same.

But nobody remembered what Ginger did other than she danced with Fred.

Nobody remembered the countless "It" girls over time who didn't make mistakes but just lived. "It" girls had been shoved into boxes and forced on medication and into family dramas that tore them apart.

The only time those girls were mentioned was when they were a case study for the next "It" girl.

I would one day fall, just like the one before me, and the one before that. I would laugh too loudly, wear a dress too short or too long. I would be too uppity, too political, not political enough. I'd be too prudish by not showing my breasts in a movie, and then a whore for daring to show cleavage at a movie premiere.

Those were the realities I dealt with every day, and I tried to push them away.

In this past month, I had been able to pretend. I had

been with Everett, and things had made sense. But that wasn't my reality; I had to remember that.

So now I was alone in my little gray cabin, and my two suitcases and carry-ons were ready to go. I had a couple of hours until Trace would whisk me out the back to a private plane, and then I would be gone forever. From the Wilders and the mania I had brought to them.

I was so afraid I wasn't going to be able to say goodbye the way that I needed to.

I wasn't sure exactly what that meant.

There was a soft knock on the door, and I knew who it was before I even checked the readout on my phone.

I let out a breath, looked through the peephole to double-check, and let Everett in.

"I see you're all packed." He looked down at the luggage at my feet, but I wanted to hurl something, to curl in a ball and cry. I wanted to do everything that was counterproductive to what I needed to do to remain strong and protect him.

"We always knew I would have to leave soon. I hadn't expected it to be like this, but perhaps, in some ways, I did."

He closed the door behind him, shaking his head. "You are just going to go. Just like that."

I pressed my lips together, holding in a sob. Crying

wasn't going to help anybody here. I needed to be strong. Walking away from him was going to be the hardest thing I ever did; I didn't want to make it any harder on him than I had to. He had been through enough as it was. I didn't want him to go through anything more.

"Of course, I'm going to go, Everett. I was always going to leave. This isn't a surprise. But those cameras out there? The people hounding your family and your guests and your way of living? They're not going to leave until I do. And they might not even leave right away, because they'll want to know why I was here. They aren't going to believe that I was here to relax."

"You're just going to leave me?" he whispered and then cursed under his breath. "I didn't mean to say that." He began to pace, the frustration wafting off him echoing mine. "Bethany, we have something. Don't you see that? I know this isn't what you were looking for when you came here. But don't you think that what we have is worth the chance?"

My heart shattered right there and then, but I had to piece it back together. I couldn't hurt him. Not any more than he was already going to be once the press got his name. And they would. They always did. There were no secrets when it came to my life. Those were the consequences of my job and the life of luxury. The one that I worked and strived and bled for.

But Everett hadn't signed up for this, so I would not force him into it. I would not let him be part of it.

"I don't know what to do. I don't know how to make this better. Walking away is the answer. I came here to breathe. To hide. And I did, but now I can't do that anymore."

"And you can't be with me anymore."

I growled. "That's not what I'm saying."

"It sure damn well looks like it's what you're saying. Your bags are packed, and you're just going to leave. Without a real goodbye?"

"I'm not leaving for a couple of hours. I was going to say goodbye. I promise you. I wasn't just going to leave."

"Like I did before."

I wanted to throw something. I wasn't that person. "You said goodbye to me before. And then the world literally shattered around you. I forgave you for never calling me. For never reaching out. You *literally* forgot me. Now I understand. But we aren't those people anymore. I can't bring you into my life. Don't you under-stand that? They will ruin you. They will look into every corner of your family, your past. They will uncover whatever they can, and they will harm the Wilders. I love it here, Everett." *I love you.* "I don't want to ruin this place. I don't want to ruin you. So it's better for everyone that I just leave."

"It's not better for everyone. It's not better for you. Not better for me."

"You're saying that I don't know what's good for me?" I asked, knowing I was deliberately misinterpreting him.

"No, I'm saying that you don't get to make my choices. We can make this work. You don't have to walk away right now. We can handle anything. We came back together after all this time. After a literal explosion took my memories of you. But I've got you back. Yes, I'm a mess. But we can make this work. I promise you."

Then his lips were on mine, and I wanted to believe.

He kept kissing me, pressing me against the wall, each step backward a temptation I couldn't say no to. I kissed him back, sliding my hands down his body.

He slid his hands over mine, cupping my breasts, then down the soft jersey dress I wore. When he slid his palms up my thighs, below my dress, I shuddered, kissing him harder. He kissed my neck, down my throat, over my shoulders. He was rough and yet soft at the same time.

As if this was a plea and a goodbye all rolled into one.

Tears slid down my face as he slowly slid down my panties, cupping me, playing with me. Teasing me.

I kept kissing him, wanting this to be forever. Wanting this to be real.

And it was, but this felt far more like a goodbye than I ever wanted it to be.

And then my legs were around him and he was pressed against me, both of us taking in sharp breaths as we looked at each other.

"Bethany. I need you."

I nodded tightly and then he was inside me, both of us moving quickly, needy, unyielding. He was thick and hard. And all I could do was breathe, try to keep hold of him. Because if I let go it would be over.

He kept kissing me, pressing into me. When he slid his thumb over my clit, I came. I clamped down around him, kissing him hard, putting everything I had of me into him. And then he came, both of us shaking.

He whispered my name, kissing the tears away from my cheeks.

I wanted this to be forever. I wanted this to be a promise, a chance.

But we were standing there in my foyer, still mostly dressed, with his come sliding down my thigh.

This was reality.

He had marked me. I wanted to be his.

He kissed me again, and the tears kept coming.

"I need to go, Everett."

"I know you do. But you don't have to leave us behind."

I wanted to believe him. I was so close to believing him. I just didn't know how he could remain unscathed and be with me.

I swallowed hard without saying anything and led him to the bathroom. We cleaned each other up, both of us silent. This was more of a goodbye than I wanted it to be.

"How would this work, Everett? Your job and your family are here. Are you ready to be a celebrity's boyfriend? Because they won't be kind. I love my job. I love acting and meeting people and creating stories. I love touching the viewers' hearts and their minds and making them think. I love making them laugh and cry and feel every emotion. But I don't love everything that comes with my job. I don't love the fact that it would hurt you. I don't want to be the cause of your pain."

He cupped my face, pressing his forehead to mine. "You don't have to have the weight of the world on your shoulders. My heart is yours, Bethany. It doesn't matter what the press says, what they think they know. They can't break us."

I let out a breath, not knowing what to do. But then

my phone rang. I frowned, looking down at the readout. I'd missed a number of calls when I was with Everett just now. I hadn't even heard it ring.

"I have to take this. It's my agent. She's called four times."

Worry crawled up my spine as Everett nodded tightly and stepped back.

"Hello? I'm sorry I was away from my phone."

"Bethany. I need you to sit down."

The controlled worry and panic in her voice was something I had never heard from her before. She was strong and had handled my career for years. Had handled the career of people who had gone through hell. And yet she sounded pained.

"What is it, Maxine?"

"Somebody leaked something online. I'm so sorry, Bethany. We're doing everything we can with our lawyers. But it's bad."

I froze, my eyes going wide as Everett looked at me. He could hear Maxine's voice through the phone and stared directly at me. I reached out, gripping his hand. I needed to steady myself and knew he wouldn't let me fall, even if that thought was a selfish one.

"What happened, Maxine?"

"Somebody leaked a video. Of you and Dallas. It's a private video, Bethany. It doesn't even look like you knew you were being recorded. But it's a three-minute-long video. And while Dallas is mostly covered up, you are not. I'm so sorry, Bethany."

I heard the words as if they were in an echo chamber. As if all of the air had been sucked out of the room, my pulse pumping loudly in my ears. Bile rose in my throat, and I was teetering on the edge of an abyss that I wasn't even aware existed.

My knees gave out and then Everett was there, holding me close. He put the phone on speaker.

"Maxine? It's Everett. What the hell just happened?"

Maxine cursed, something she never did with me. "Everett. I'm sorry. Not only did somebody leak a video that we are trying to deal with, but they also brought up your name and are alleging that you have been with Bethany since before she and Dallas broke up. They are dragging the Wilders in the press. We're contacting Eli to try to do some damage control, but you're going to need a publicity team." Maxine sucked in a deep breath and continued. "It appears that Dallas did this. From what we can tell, he's the one who had the video. We think it's in retaliation."

I couldn't keep up, she kept speaking, but I held out my hand as if she could see me. "In retaliation for what?"

Was that my voice? No, that icy-cold, emotionless voice couldn't be me. And yet I knew it was. I'd said the words. They'd escaped my own lips, and yet it didn't feel like me.

"He lost his role in the next action film. He's been recast. His coke problem is now a media joke, but is being buried. *By this.* We're doing all we can, Bethany, but it's bad. You should come home. We can keep you safe here."

She continued to say things and I nodded along, even though she couldn't see me. I whispered my answers, and I knew Trace and the others would be here soon to take me to the airport.

I wasn't breaking inside. Because to break, there had to have been something whole to begin with. I was just a hollow vessel of nothingness.

Someone had taken my private moments and put them online.

As soon as Maxine hung up, I took the phone back and opened up the browser app.

"Bethany, don't do it."

"No. I need to see what they've seen. I need to know."

Again, that didn't sound like my voice. Everett looked worried. So sweet. And yet his family needed a publicist because they were going to drag his name through the mud because he cared for me. Because he was there for me.

This was what Bethany Cole did. She burned bridges and never looked back. She ruined men, and she walked away. She was just an icy bitch, they said.

Perhaps that was true. Though to leave those marks, you had to be someone.

And I was no one.

In the end, the video was easy to see. I just had to type B, and it was the first thing that popped up. I didn't even need to type my name. I was the first search term for the letter B.

It was as if I were witnessing someone else watching the video. I wasn't present in my own body. But I had been present when I was making love to my boyfriend. He had recorded me. I hadn't even known the camera was there. But he had. Because he winked as it as he thrust into me. As he took me and I asked for more. As all of me, every inch of my body, was shown to the world. A body that I had wanted to remain *mine*. I had nudity clauses in my contracts because I wanted my body to be mine. I respected everybody who made their own choices for their own bodies. But my choice had been taken from me.

This was it. There was no going back. What else had he taken from me? What else had been done?

The comments made me want to throw up. So many people had been ready for me to fall.

I was no longer America's Princess. I was America's Prostitute.

I couldn't focus. All I could do was see Everett's name in some of the comments. As if they *knew* he had to have been the reason for this. They knew so much, but they didn't know anything.

The violation was something I couldn't even let out into the world.

How could I put those words together to form a sentence?

"Bethany?"

Everett touched me when he spoke. He stood there but didn't look down at the phone. Had he seen? Had he watched with me? Had he seen what had been taken from me?

Why would he want to touch me? I was dirty. I was used. I was broken.

I hated those words.

A small part of me was screaming. Screaming and yelling at me that this wasn't my fault. That I had consented to sex but not to recording. I was not doing anything wrong in that video. And yet somebody had plastered it online because they thought they had the right.

The man I had trusted had betrayed me in more ways than I could count.

I was screaming these things at myself, and all I could do was try to push that away because everything hurt in this twisted echo of who I had been.

"I need to go. I need to go home."

"Bethany. It's not your fault. I'll kill him for this."

I shook my head, the numbness settling in. The numbness would help.

"Don't hurt him. If I thought hurting him, bruising him, killing him, would do anything, I would do it myself. But the world still loves him. He's a drug addict who prostituted me out for the world, and I didn't even know it. The world still loves him. I'm sorry for what they're doing to your family. I'm sorry I didn't leave soon enough for this not to touch you."

"Bethany. Don't blame yourself. This is not on you. My family can handle this. I can handle this. Let me help you."

"No. It's over." There were no more tears. I didn't need to cry for this. Because in order to cry, I needed to be a person. And I was just a three-minute video. There was nothing left of me to bare. "This isn't your world, Everett. And you were thrust into it because of me. I need to go. Trace will be here soon to take me home. My team will do what they can to protect you. Soon the media will forget the Wilders. They will move on to something else. Something else I did. You will be safe. Just keep your family safe."

I pushed past him and he reached out, gripping my hand. I flinched, pulling away. I didn't mean to hurt him. I wasn't flinching at him. But it was so hard. If I let him touch me, I would crumble, I would break, and I couldn't. I needed to be strong to walk out of this house. To walk away from him.

I saw the hurt on his face. I couldn't fix it.

I couldn't fix anything.

Tears threatened, but I pushed them back. The tears would just be a weapon, and I couldn't be that person anymore.

"I'm sorry. I have to go."

"You don't. You don't have to go. I don't know how to fix this, but I'll stand by you. I promise you. Don't push me away."

"Let me do it. For both our sakes."

And then Trace was there, and Frank, and they held Everett back as I got in the back of the SUV. I didn't remember the car ride. I didn't remember getting on the private plane. I came back to myself when I was settling into the seat as I stared out the window vacancy, wondering if there was anything left.

I ignored the calls from Lark, my team. I would get

back to them soon. I just needed a few more minutes to piece myself together. To find a semblance of Bethany Cole. Because once I did, we would formulate a plan to get through this.

I would be me, but Everett would be him.

In the end, I would have no one.

Just like I was meant to. I would be safe.

I didn't need to make another mistake.

I didn't have anything else left to lose.

# Chapter Fifteen

Bethany

"We have the interview and photo shoot tomorrow with *Event Horizon*. I have always found the title of that publication a little daunting. However, it was already set up for next month, and they had to move it ahead. They want to talk about the movie. That's what they promised us. So that is what we're going to do." Maxine paced some more as she went through the lineup of my next few weeks.

I was working. Interviews. Training. Vocal coaches. Dance coaches for a single scene that would probably be cut from the movie anyway. Countless things that I had to do to keep busy.

All while pretending that I wasn't dying inside.

The media storm hadn't quite died down. It wouldn't happen for a while, and yet in the world of 24-hour news, the next celebrity breakup had already happened on the heels of my worst nightmare.

Infidelity, secret children, multiple nanny adulterers. All of that rolled up into one tidy headline, and I was now on page two. The bottom of the fold. My humiliation, torments, and personal life were now only second fiddle, at least as far as the internet was concerned.

I hadn't handled my social media in years, but my team dug through the filth, trolls, and constant harassment to find goodness. They were tougher than I was, because it wasn't truly them that were being crudely threatened.

The reporters were still camped outside of our neighborhood, but it wasn't only for me. A religious cult member, turned celebrity, turned once again religious cult member lived three houses down, and they were also in the news cycle.

"Are you okay?" Maxine asked. Once again, I heard the worry in her tone. That bothered me more than anything. Because Maxine didn't break down. She didn't sound worried. She got things done, that's why I hired her and loved her even when I hated her.

But she was worried, which made it worse for me.

"I'm fine."

"You will be. That's what I'm here for."

I snorted. "If you already knew the answer, then why did you ask?"

"Because I have to. Because I want to. I'm sorry that your bodily autonomy was taken from you. That your consent was taken from you. I hate that this is part of our daily lives, that people think that they can just throw it in the news and you can move on. It will come out of the woodwork every single time you have a movie because that is what they do. But what I do is try to fix the narrative. My job is to protect you. Not just your brand. *You.* I failed to do that with that asshole, and once we get through these next weeks, if you want to fire me, fine. But know I am going to do all in my power to make sure that this doesn't happen again. I can't fix it. But I can make the landing not as harsh."

I stared at Maxine, shocked. She never spoke like this. She was never personal or righteous. It was always work and making the right step forward. I wanted to break down in tears, so instead, I reached forward and gave her a fierce hug.

She didn't pat me on the back. Instead, she let out a breath and began muttering about babying celebrities.

I just held her tightly before she finally patted me on the back and sighed.

"Yes, yes. I love you too. How's that?"

I grinned, despite the situation. "Well then. You love me. My day is complete."

"I know it's everything that you've been waiting for." Maxine looked away and cleared her throat. "Speaking of love..."

I held up my hand. "Don't bring him up again."

"The Wilders didn't put out a statement, but their company's publicist is really good at their job." She pointed to her table, and I saw a picture of the retreat, the place that had been my home, my oasis.

Somehow they had got all six brothers, along with their sister, hugging and laughing in front of the inn. Their team members were behind them, all holding up glasses of wine and random plates of cheese. Some had margaritas, some just water. But everyone was laughing, with a pregnant Kendall leaning into Evan. A smiling Alexis looking up at Eli with stars in her eyes.

Joy was tucked into Elijah's side.

Elliot and East flanked the group, with Elliot beaming like a golden retriever, practically bouncing on his feet in the stationary photo. East glared at the camera but still came off rugged and charming.

And dab in the center was Everett. He wasn't smiling. In fact, I wasn't even sure the world coudln't see the torment in his gaze.

The torment that I had put in his face.

He had his arms folded over his chest, but I saw pride there. Pride in his family and everything that they had done. That was the man that I had left.

The man that I loved.

Underneath the joyous and charismatic photo showing just a glimpse of exactly who they were, was a headline that brought me to tears.

***Taming of the Wilders: how a family fought for our country and are now making a home of their own and for guests in our hill country.***

I swallowed hard and nearly reached out to touch Everett's face.

"They did a feature?"

"Yes. They don't mention you. They don't mention what happened. And that's good." Maxine cleared her throat. "They offered. They offered to defend you. But I said that we weren't commenting at this time other than to respect your privacy. So they wrote about their family. About what they're doing. Trying to show their small part of the world they made into a home. Memories. It's good PR. Nobody's asking about the man in the center of the photo and his connection to you. Not in this piece."

"They're braver than me. They came together as a family and made things work. Wrote something. And here I am trying to move on as if it hadn't happened."

"Do you want to make a statement? Do you want to go on the late-night circuit and daytime circuit to clear your name? No, that's not the right word is it? Just speak your truth."

I pressed my lips together, then stared out my window at the view that I had once loved. "Dallas took something from me. I hadn't even realized I had given it to him. He took much more than just my pride when he cheated on me. I have an idea. To write something. But it seems silly in retrospect. People are dying all over the world. Real things are happening. And yes, I lost part of myself, but will people listen?"

Maxine reached out and squeezed my shoulder before letting her hand drop. "I think somebody needs to hear. Even if it's just one person...they do. And maybe you need to write it."

There wasn't much left to say after that, and she left me alone in my giant house with its echoing walls, and I wondered how I done this to myself.

My intercom buzzed and I looked over at the readout.

"Ms. Cole?"

"Trace," I said, after I pressed the button on my flat touchpad. "You know to call me Bethany."

"I'm in the mood to call you Ms. Cole. You have a guest."

I stiffened. "I don't want to talk to anybody."

"I know. But you might want to talk to him."

I looked at the screen again and saw his face. Everett. How was he here? He couldn't be here. I had to stop thinking about him. But he was here. In LA. He was supposed to be in Texas, keeping safe, keeping away from the cameras. Then he just walked right into the lion's den. What was this man thinking?

Angry now, I pressed the buzzer to let him in.

I looked down at my soft linen pants that billowed around my legs and my gray cropped top that made me look like I was taking the day off, when in reality, I had thrown clothes on and not cared what I looked like.

My hair was piled on top of my head, and I wore no makeup, just tinted sunscreen like I did every morning.

I wasn't the Bethany Cole everybody knew, but then again, did they know me?

I pushed away those thoughts of self-reflection that were far too deep right then and opened the door to find him standing there alone. He had a duffel on one shoulder, his hair was disheveled. I noticed the hat in his free hand, the sunglasses perched on the tip of his nose.

He wore jeans with holes at the knees, a gray T-shirt with a bleach stain at the bottom.

His muscles were on full display, as was his ink, and he looked gorgeous. Rugged, handsome, no longer mine.

"Everett. What are you doing here?"

"I figured we needed to talk. I wanted to give you space before, but now, let's talk."

"I don't think there's anything to talk about. I saw the article. I didn't read it, but Maxine told me what it was about. I'm so sorry you and your family have gone through this."

He shook his head. "Can I come in? Sweetheart, we can have this conversation on your porch if you need to. I will come in if you'll let me. I won't invade your space. But I figured this wasn't a good conversation for the phone. And I wanted to see you."

Goosebumps pricked my flesh, and I swallowed hard. "Of course, come in. Sorry for leaving you standing out there."

His lips quirked into a smile as he walked in, his boots squeaking slightly on the marble.

"Want me to take off my shoes?" he asked, a brow raised.

I shook my head. "You don't have to. I don't in the house, but you know that."

He met my gaze and it was if I was looking at the man who knew everything and yet a stranger all wrapped up into one. "I know." He let out a breath. "I would ask how you're doing, but I've seen what the news tells me. I'm sorry. I'm so damn sorry about everything that happened. I wish I could've gone with you. To here, at least. So you weren't alone on that flight."

"I have my team." It sounded hollow, and he gave me a sad smile.

"I know. I know you had them. I just wish you had me, too. But I hadn't been strong enough to not let you go."

"Everett, don't do this."

"All I'm doing is asking you to try. He took something from you. The world is trying to do the same. I don't want to be that person. I know it's painful and horrible and nothing I can say can make it better. But I want to be by your side for this. I know you say you can handle it, but I cannot. I've held a lot in my life, Bethany, and I don't want you to go through this alone."

"Everett. You can't be with me just to take care of me. That's not how things work."

"You're right. We can take care of each other. We can be there for each other. That's the whole point.

233

Those people can print what they think they know about you. They think that they know us. But they don't. I know you, Bethany. I know the parts of you that you shared with me, and I want to know more. I want to spend my days learning more."

"They'll tear you apart just like they're trying to do to me."

"That's right. Trying. Because they aren't succeeding. They can't tear you apart. I hate saying the word strong, you know that. But you're so damn strong, Bethany. I can't fix what the paparazzi does. What society does. But I can fix this connection that we have. I can make sure you know your worth. Because you have it. You've always known it. But you keep forgetting. Because of what this world of ours keeps doing. You're not alone. I promise you. You're not alone."

I pressed my lips together, ignoring the tears threatening.

"I know you want to push me away again. Because you think it's going to protect me. But it just hurts us both. I love you, Bethany."

I pressed my hands to my lips, shaking my head. "Don't. Don't say that. You can't love me."

He finally set down his duffel bag and then stepped forward and cupped my face. "Bethany. I love you. I love that we had a second chance. A second chance I didn't even realize could happen. The greatest sin I ever committed was letting you go, to think that there was no way out. That you were alone. It's what I've done to myself all these years, but I'm not going to do it to you. I love you so much."

"Everett."

"You don't have to say it back to me. I know that I have no idea what this world of yours entails. I will learn. I will do whatever I can to take that on because all that matters is I want to be with you. And I know you want to be with me."

"Everett, I want to be with you. But what if I hurt you?"

"You can't hurt me. The world can try, but we have each other. We will learn who we are together. I just want a chance, Bethany. I don't want the outside world to push us apart. If you don't want me for me? Let me know. I'll walk away. I won't be like that asshole. But know that I love you."

I let the tears fall. I hadn't even realized I moved until I was cupping his face. He hadn't shaved in a while, his beard a little rough against my palm. I had missed this. Missed him.

"I didn't expect you, Everett. I...I don't know what's going to happen next. My life is in a whirlwind right now, with so much going on. But I love you. I'm so scared. I love you."

I said the words, and I hadn't meant to.

In all my years with Dallas, I had never said the words to him. I would say maybe that was the problem, but in the end, the problem was Dallas.

Everett smiled then, and kissed me softly. "You have no idea how good it feels to hear that."

I shook my head and stepped away. "If we do this, then it is going to change everything. The world already thinks they know your name, and if they see you with me? They're going to want to know more. I don't know what my responses are yet for everything that happened. Other things have taken over the news cycle, but as soon as I step out on the circuit again to promote my next movie? It's going to come up. What they did to me. What they saw. You. Everything. And I'm formulating a plan, but it is not going to be easy. They're going to try to hurt you. To hurt us. And I left to make sure that didn't happen."

"Then you tell me what to do. Unless you want me to figure it out with you. Like I said, I might be out of my element, but I want to figure it out with you."

"It's not going to be easy."

"Of course, it isn't. Nothing worthwhile ever is. But, Bethany? You know your worth. You know what those people saw? That was a private moment. That was *your* moment. I haven't looked." He met my gaze. "I swear. None of my family has. That was for you. You did not give consent, so we're not going to cross that line. Ever."

I wiped my face. "Honestly, it never crossed my mind that you would. I guess that should've told me something."

"I guess it should have. So, tell me what you want to do next."

"What about your job?"

"I can do much of it remotely. But I have the next couple of weeks to be with you. The Wilders have worked hard to make this happen. We're a well-oiled machine." He knocked on the wooden table next to me. "Just in case."

My lips twitched. "I have a photo shoot and an interview tomorrow. That is, after I talk with the authorities again about another stalker email." I held up my hand. "It's the same email as before, but they re-sent it. As if making sure that I knew they were watching. I don't know what's going on, but it feels like it's one thing too much. Tomorrow, the interview is supposed to be for the movie, but you never know. I don't know what to say, but I have a few ideas."

"I would love to hear them."

"I've never really had anyone to listen before that I wasn't paying," I said with a roll of my eyes.

"That's a lie. You have Lark."

I pressed my lips together, my tears threatening again. "I can tell Lark a lot of things. But on this subject, I didn't want to hurt her." It wasn't my secret to tell, so he nodded and held out his arms. And somehow, he was holding me, and I was hugging him and laughing, wondering exactly what would happen.

Because I knew love didn't answer all. Love didn't conquer all.

Despite the movies I was in, and the books that I loved, sometimes love wasn't enough.

I didn't want to feel like I was just fooling myself. But tomorrow, the real world beckoned. My version of reality.

And I had to find out if I was strong enough.

Or if I was bringing Everett down with me.

# Chapter Sixteen

### Everett

I only had a small idea of what Bethany did during the day for her job, and she wasn't even on set. Today was just the prep for set and an interview and photo shoot. A single day in her life, where I was trying to prove that I could hack it.

No, that wasn't quite right. Because while I did want to prove something, it was more that I just wanted to be with *her*.

I still couldn't believe that I had jumped on a plane, with my brothers practically pushing me there. And standing on her doorstep, waiting for her to let me in, under the glaring gaze of Trace, her bodyguard, hadn't been easy. But here I was, trying to make this work.

"Okay, bend your elbow slightly, chin up, there, Bethany, you're beautiful. You're a natural."

I could tell at the moment that Bethany was trying not to roll her eyes, considering this photographer so far had instructed Bethany to do many contradicting things that didn't make much sense and at first had her bending over random chairs backward, trying to look avant-garde. The photographer had then deleted all those photos, saying they weren't worth the screen they were printed on, whatever that meant. Now Bethany sat in a throne-like chair, chin up, leaning against one arm, staring directly at the camera.

Fierce, intelligent, and mine.

Not that I said that out loud.

Another staffer walked by, gave me a curious glance, and I just smiled and went back to my computer, doing my own work while I watched.

Everybody was curious about the man that had come with Bethany Cole to her interview. And yet they all knew. They'd seen the news stories, the trashy headlines.

They knew why this no one named Everett Wilder was now with Bethany at work.

The news would spread, but Bethany said she was prepared for that.

Because it was time for her to control her narrative. To set herself back into her own story rather than the one the world thought that they needed to tell about her.

And I was falling more and more in love with her every single day. Her strength, her essence. Everything. She was everything.

"Can I get you some water?" Tonya, Bethany's assistant, asked from my side. I had met Tonya the day before at Bethany's house. When we were introduced she had squealed, clapped her hands, and thrown her arms around my neck, hugging me tight, welcoming me to Bethany's team.

Bethany had just rolled her eyes and laughed, though I had tried to keep up. Apparently, Tonya was in my corner. I liked that. Trace, who had once been in my corner, was now a little hesitant. I didn't blame him. There was a lot to keep her safe from, and if somebody came at Bethany, I would be pushed to the side and Bethany would be the one being taken care of. I wholeheartedly agreed with that sentiment, so I didn't mind. But if I was the one that put Bethany in danger? Trace said he would end me right then and there.

I didn't know if threatening murder was the way to

go, but I honestly believed the man with the way he was glaring at me.

I hadn't met Bethany's manager yet, but she said I would soon. I wasn't quite sure what to make of the other woman, other than she was ready to take me down a peg if I hurt Bethany. I didn't mind because Bethany was number one in my eyes.

Maxine, the final main member of her inner team, had only met me through video chat. She had narrowed her eyes at me, nodded tightly, and told Bethany that she would see me soon. I didn't quite know what that meant, but Bethany looked relieved. Without knowing it, I had crossed a goalpost that I hadn't even realized was in front of me.

And that was just Bethany's inner workings. There were her publicity teams, her makeup artists, her personal shopper, and a thousand other people that helped her style and get ready for events like this. I had known the Bethany at the cabin—sweet, tired, and yet still hard-working.

I had also known the one that I had danced with at a club in LA and had fallen for before I went off to Afghanistan. Those were the Bethanys that I knew. But I was learning this one too.

I loved her all the more for it.

She had a thousand people asking her for things, on her payroll, needing her for something. And I knew right then that my job was to be the person *not* in that line. Who didn't depend on her for my livelihood.

She was mine just like I was hers. But our relationship was going to be different.

I just didn't know exactly what the dynamics were going to be, considering I was a fish out of water here, and we lived in completely different worlds.

But we wanted to try.

"I'm good," I said, shaking myself out of my reverie. "Thanks, though, Tonya."

She beamed at me. "No problem. They should be at the interview part soon, though the photographer will probably take photos during. So don't worry. You've got this."

"I'm not sure that I have anything to do about this. She's the one who has this."

"You're right. She does. I'm glad that you know that." She gave me a brisk nod and then went off to help Bethany with something else.

Trace came up to my side then, his gaze on everyone else, not me. I figured that was a good thing because he was keeping Bethany secure, and apparently, I wasn't the threat.

"Don't fuck this up. Because she needs you just like you need her."

I blinked and looked at the other man, but he was already stepping away, going back to his duties. I would've thought it had been my imagination, but no, he had been right here.

And he might be on my side. That was interesting.

"Okay, Bethany. Let's just talk. I know you have a lot of things to talk about. Let's chat about the movie first. Are you excited to be working with Bowen Bridges?" she asked, beginning the interview.

I remembered Bowen Bridges was a veteran actor with an Oscar, Tony, and a few other things under his belt. I liked him in his movies, and I knew he was the romantic interest for Bethany in her upcoming one. I would just have to get over the fact that she would be kissing another man on screen. It was her job, and honestly, I wasn't going to feel jealous.

I couldn't. Not when she would come home to me.

And damn, wasn't that a wonderful thought.

Bethany smiled, looking strong and professional, like she was the queen of the world.

Or at least *my* world.

"I so admire Bowen. He's brilliant, and I feel like I'll learn so much even though I've been doing this job what feels like forever." She laughed. "Of course, I'm not really supposed to mention that I've been doing this for years. I'm supposed to be a doe-eyed, sweet teenager, right?" She winked as she said it, and the reporter and everyone else laughed.

She would have them eating out of the palm of her hand, and I couldn't help but admire her for it. I knew she was damn scared. While the reporter said she would just talk about the movie, we all knew that was a lie. This was her first interview since everything had happened. People wanted to know how she felt about the recording. About the breakup. About the cheating. The drugs. Me.

They'd been clamoring for her. And she had kept silent, perhaps to her detriment, at least according to some.

I just knew that this was Bethany's choice. That was the only thing that mattered.

The reporter continued to ask questions, then leaned forward. "Okay, just between you and me."

Bethany laughed softly. "I think that's not quite true, considering the cameras on me, as are the eyes of around a hundred people."

The reporter waved her hand. "Oh, fine. You do not have to answer this, I will move on in a blink if you want. But...I see you have a very attractive bearded man behind me, looking at you with adoration. He looks kind, sweet, and not as much out of his element as I thought he would. So, tell me more about Everett Wilder."

I froze, just now aware that Tonya was at my side, as if for support. I was grateful for that. I would do whatever Bethany wanted. If she wanted me in the limelight, I would do it. If she wanted me off to the side where I could live my normal life, fine.

I would figure it out. I had almost died before. Almost lost everything. I *had* lost part of myself. I wasn't going to be hesitant anymore. Not when it came to taking what I wanted, living my life.

"I'm finding my peace," Bethany answered. "With who I want to be. With who I am. What I want." She looked over at me and winked, and I saw the camera flash as they captured the photo.

"Is your peace with Everett Wilder?" The reporter asked again, intrigue in her voice.

"It could be. I'm figuring that out. Is that not the whole point of discovery? Some parts are just for me. And that's okay. We all deserve parts that are just ours. I'm figuring out who I am after others tried to put labels on me. I can't change what others think of me. Only what I think about myself."

"You're right. Others want to put labels on you. And you have been quite silent about what those labels are. You have a right to that. But is there something that you want to say right now? I will ask the question—Anything you want to say for yourself? Because you deserve the right to say something or not at all. So, in your own words, how are you?"

The reporter had been joking at first, laughter in her tone as she eased Bethany into the interview. That had been professional and had indeed begun with work.

Bethany met my gaze, smiled, and looked straight back at the camera, her chin raised, not defiantly, but confident.

"Everyone knows what they saw. Or rather, what they thought they saw. I had sex with the man I chose. A man I was in a monogamous relationship with. I consented to have sex with him. But I did not consent to be recorded." She let out a breath, her gaze narrowing. "I did not consent to my face being plastered every-where, other people asking questions that they had no right to ask. I did not bring them into my bedroom. Or anywhere else. If I had wanted myself to be displayed in that manner, I would have done it myself. I would've made that choice. But others made that choice for me."

"I'm sorry about that."

Bethany gave the other woman a wry smile. "I know

you personally are. But not everybody is. They want the headlines. They want to see me knocked down a peg. I wasn't quite sure how I found myself on top of the ladder, as it were. I make movies because I want to create characters. I want to explore how these characters react to everyday things, or aliens coming from outer space and attacking the world. I want to see who I can be when I portray these people. I want to entertain, make people laugh, cry, have their hearts ache. Everything. That is my role. And I am blessed to do it. Blessed that I seemed to have connected with some." She let out a breath, then looked back at the camera. "I seem to also connect with others who had things done to them without their consent. Whether it is revenge porn, as this is, or other more horrific things. There are people who did not give their consent. And here I am, not sure what I will do next. Will I sue, as so many people are saying I should? That is up to me. But I do not want this happening to anyone else. I do not want anyone else losing their power, their voice. I lost part of myself when I was hiding on their terms. But these are my terms. I will live the way I want to. Be with who I want to be with, how I want to live. I am blessed to do this job. I work fourteen to twenty hours a day sometimes, and I know that I'm privileged. So, I will do all in my power to use that privilege to help others."

I knew I loved Bethany Cole, but damn if I didn't just fall in love with her even more.

"And what about Dallas? What do you say to him?" the reporter asked. I could hear the tears in her voice. Apparently, Bethany had said something that touched her, just like I knew it touched every single damn person in this room.

Bethany shook her head, a frown on her face. "I hope that man gets healthy. That he finds his own peace. Because I am finding mine." She looked at me then, and I knew the interview was over.

Bethany Cole had taken one step into the future. I was so damn proud of her. She had found her voice, taken her step. Just like I was doing. Fighting for what we wanted.

When the interview ended, she continued to speak with the reporter, and a few others, before she came over to me. I closed down my computer and stood up from the chair, my back aching.

"I don't have any words. You took them all." I smiled as I said it, and then she threw her arms around my shoulders and kissed me soundly on the mouth. I caught her as she jumped, wrapping my own arms around her waist, bringing her to me.

I knew people were probably taking photos. There

was no hiding this. But I kissed her hard and then pressed my forehead to hers once we were done.

"So, I guess we're public?" I whispered.

"I think I'm tired of hiding everything all the time. We'll figure this out. Together."

I smiled, brushed her hair from her face, and laughed as Tonya pulled my hand back.

"Stop it. She still has one more thing to do today that requires hair and that makeup."

"Of course, we can't hurt the makeup." Bethany rolled her eyes, even as she fist-bumped the makeup artist.

I blushed. "You really just have to tell me what to do."

"See, son, that's exactly how you make it in a relationship," Trace added.

I snorted. "You would really fit in with my brothers."

"Trace and the Wilders?" Bethany asked. "That would be fun."

Trace snorted and went back to work.

"I need to do a few more things. Then we can go get dinner? I know it's been a long day. And I know everything has happened pretty fast. It'll be nice to relax."

"Can I cook you something? That way, you don't have to be under scrutiny?" I asked.

Bethany went to her toes and kissed my cheek. "I

don't want to hide you away, but maybe that would be a good idea for now."

"Anything you want. And that means I get some work done and annoy my brothers because it's what I do."

I kissed her softly, ignoring Tonya's glare, and went back to work, only pausing when my phone rang.

I frowned as I saw Maddie's name on the readout. "Hey there, Maddie. Everything going okay at the winery? Did I not send that latest report?" I had a headache, but only a slight one. I knew the headaches were never going to go away fully, but I was doing what I should—speaking to my therapist, going to physical therapy, trying to relax, and being open.

I was working. At least as far as I could.

"Everett?" Maddie asked, her voice breaking.

I stiffened, everything going on alert. "What is it, Maddie? Is everyone okay? The babies? Is it the babies?" Worry for Kendall and Evan shot through me.

"No, the babies are fine. Everett. You need to come home."

"What's wrong, Maddie?" I asked, and Bethany must've heard the alarm in my tone because she moved to me, ignoring something one of the staffers was saying.

"It's Joy. There's been an accident."

"Is she okay? Maddie? What is going on?"

"She's dead, Everett. Joy is gone. Elijah needs you." She paused, a sob breaking through. "We all need you. Come home, Everett."

And with that, my world once again shifted on its axis.

# Chapter Seventeen

Everett

My family was no stranger to death. We had lived it day in and day out for two decades. From the first moment Eli put on his dress blues, we knew things would change forever. An irrevocable promise, bound in fate, sorrow, and change.

We had all followed him. All but Eliza.

Our younger sister had married someone who had joined our path. She had found her own strength, her own way of life and service. And when her husband died, it was the first stone cast.

We had each lost someone in war or battle. We had lost people to IEDs, gunfire, and explosions.

I could still see the blood of my best friends on my hands as I tried to stagger my way through the wet sand, wet from the blood pouring from my head wound.

I could still taste the coppery scent on my tongue.

And I knew every single family member in this room had their own terrors running unending in their mind.

But we worked in battles. We wanted to serve our country.

We were no longer in the military.

Loss, death, and heartache weren't supposed to hit like this, out of the blue, anymore.

We had made this home of ours, despite the constant ache and need and strength it took to make it. We had confined ourselves in a sanctuary from the pain and memories. From the blood and terror of who we'd been.

And yet, we hadn't run fast enough. We hadn't built the walls to keep us safe high enough.

"Everett?"

I looked over at Bethany. She slid her hand into mine.

"I'm sorry. Did you say something?" Her eyes darted to mine, studying my face before she shook her head. "You were lost in your own thoughts. I just wanted to make sure you were okay. That your head was okay."

I smiled, though it didn't feel real, and I didn't feel bad about feeling how I had. I didn't worry that she was trying to keep me protected, because that's what I did for her.

"I don't have a headache. I don't feel anything."

"I don't know if that's good or bad. But if you need me, I'm here." She squeezed my hand tighter, and I nodded.

We stood in Eli's home, far away from LA. Far away from the paparazzi who had followed us all the way to the airport. Joy's death hadn't made the news. Nobody outside of our circle and Joy's circle knew she was gone or would even recognize her name.

I didn't need the world to care who I was.

I needed them to remember Joy.

The woman who had made my brother smile. Who had brought Elijah out of his shell so he relaxed more. So he acted like the man I had once known, albeit with a few more scars.

Joy had brought the world to Elijah, and now she was gone. In one freak accident. A car had run a red light and hydroplaned through the rain-slicked streets.

When it rained here, streets filled quickly, flash flooding an eager and ready problem. The water would be quickly washed away, seeping into the aquifer. But before that, it was a hazard. Something that was dangerous for anyone on the road.

They hadn't seen Joy as she crossed the street towards the restaurant, where Elijah stood waiting.

Waiting for her.

She was struck by the car and hit the pavement, and died on the scene.

The girl who my brother loved was gone.

And I didn't have any words for him. How was I supposed to tell Elijah that I was sorry? That wasn't fair. It didn't make any sense.

"I'm glad that you're here," East said as he came to my side.

I looked over at my twin and wrapped my arm around his shoulder, squeezing tightly.

East sighed and leaned against the wall. "Elijah is sitting in the office. Eli is with him. I'm surprised he let anybody in."

"How did you even get him here?" I asked. I was still trying to keep up with everything that had happened. Bethany's team had gotten us a ticket out here as quickly as possible, so I hadn't had to worry about any of that. I guess it was good to have a movie star as a girlfriend, even if you weren't sure what was happening.

Because within a few hours of Maddie's call, we were touching down in San Antonio, and then in the back of East's car as he drove us to Eli's.

Bethany had canceled all of her events for today and tomorrow, citing a death in the family.

Because it was family. She was my family, just as Joy was Elijah's.

I cursed under my breath as Bethany squeezed my hand and East gave me a look.

"We got him here because he's not thinking. Not doing anything. He wasn't next of kin, so all he could do was wait to hear updates about arrangements and all that shit from her brother. I know it's going to happen eventually. We just have to make sure that he's not alone."

"We won't let him be alone. He's our family."

"Anything you need from me. Just let me know. Sometimes my name gets through doors otherwise closed." Bethany shrugged as she said it, not the least ashamed. Not that she should be.

"I don't know what connections you would have here, but if we need them, we appreciate it," he said with a growl, and I knew the growl wasn't for her, but the situation.

"I'm not good at this. I don't know what to do for

him. What about the business? Can I help there?" Bethany asked, and I squeezed her hand.

"Maddie is handling a lot of it, but you're right. I should go talk with her. Eli and Alexis and the others have Elijah. And I know he knows that we're here. But maybe we should go take care of everything else on his plate, so he doesn't have to think about it."

"That's a good idea," Elliot said, frowning at his tablet. "Eli and Alexis will keep him here. You and I can go back to the property and do what we can with Maddie." He looked at Bethany. "You're welcome to help. I just don't know what your skills are."

"Elliot," I warned.

Elliot winced. "I'm sorry. I feel weird. Fuck. Of course, we're all having a weird day. What is wrong with me? Why do I keep saying the wrong things?"

Bethany moved to him and gripped his free hand. "Because there aren't any right things to say. People deal with grief and death in whatever way that they can. They struggle just to put one foot in front of the other. Some people need a list so they can figure out exactly what they can do before they can let everything else shatter in. So, what is it that I can do to help?"

Elliot gave her a soft smile. "I have a list. Lists, I know."

"I'll drive you guys back," East put in. "Evan is in the guest room with Kendall."

I whirled. "What's wrong?" I asked, my heart beating far too fast. Bethany put her hand on the small of my back, calming me, but only just.

"They just want to keep Kendall as calm as possible. They are nearing the end of the pregnancy, and she's having twins. So anything like that is a higher risk than normal. She's taking a nap, and honestly, I think it's just to keep Evan calm. Eliza and Beckett will be down tomorrow."

"Beckett is my sister's husband," I said to Bethany.

She nodded. "I know. You told me. Let's do this. I'm not much help here. But we can be help there."

"I hate the fact that I feel so lucky to have you," I whispered.

She smiled up at me, though it didn't reach her eyes, and she cupped my face. "Same here. We will figure it out together. I love you."

"I love you, too."

Then we left, and I had to hope that Elijah would come out of the room eventually, and I could hug my brother, and tell him that we would find a way to be okay. But I wasn't quite sure that was going to happen yet.

We made our way onto the property through security and got to work on whatever Elliot told us to. He was the planner, so I just did what I was told.

Bethany, with her spreadsheets along with Elliot, was a planner to her core, which made me happy.

I had my own job to do and picked up some of Eli's and Evan's along the way. Maddie was a force, her hair blowing in the breeze as she made her own gale moving so fast. She was doing Elijah's and Evan's job at that point, the rest of the winery picking up loose ends.

Everybody was working so hard to make sure that my brothers didn't have anything else to worry about.

Because the worst had happened. There was no coming back.

Everything just felt too heavy, too painful.

By the time we closed up everything for the evening, I was exhausted, and I knew that Bethany had to be more so.

We had taken the redeye here and hadn't really slept. Though I wasn't sure if anybody had slept.

To the outside world, the Wilder Retreat worked like a well-oiled machine. From the inside, we were breaking down, shattered into a thousand pieces as we tried to figure out the next step.

We would do it together. Even if I had no idea what to say to my brother.

"I think somebody's in your cabin, so I guess you're coming home with me."

I kissed the top of her head as she leaned into me.

"Honestly, as long as there's a bed, I'm fine."

Trace stepped forward. "We checked out your place already, we will do it again. But you guys have a good night."

I looked up at Trace and nodded at him. He had been around most of the day, working with our security branch and trying to make sure that everything was good for Bethany.

I still hadn't forgotten the notes, the threats. Or the paparazzi. But with everything else, it was all I could do to just keep her safe.

Because I did not want to go through what Elijah was going through.

"Your arm tightened around my shoulders. What's wrong, baby?" Bethany cursed. "Other than the obvious."

"I was just thinking that I have no idea what I'm supposed to do. And what I would do if I were in my brother's shoes."

"Don't think about that. You can't. All you can do is

grieve for your brother. I know that nothing will be okay for a while."

"What did I do to deserve you?" I asked, my voice barely above a whisper. We stood in my living room now, standing against one another as if we could fall asleep on our feet.

"You're just you. I think I have to ask what I did to deserve you. You were thrust into my world, and we don't even have our footing yet."

"You're in my world now. I don't think either one of us was prepared for anything."

"That sounds about right. I could use some water or something before bed. And I'm going to crash. I hope that's okay."

I smiled softly. "That sounds pretty good. I feel like nothing is reality at this point."

"I live outside of reality most days. So I understand that."

I kissed the top of her head, and we made our way to my kitchen. We turned around the corner, and I froze, grateful that Bethany was slightly behind me.

A woman with dark messy hair stood in front of us, her bangs chopped off at an odd angle, a baggy sweatshirt over her tiny frame. She had on holey jeans and sparkly flip-flops. She looked familiar, but I couldn't quite place her.

That was, until she looked up at us, and I froze.

"Cassandra?" Bethany asked, her voice breaking.

How the hell had this woman broken in here? Was this Cassandra Fox? She didn't really look like her. She didn't have on any makeup, just left-over mascara streaked from crying. She looked horrible. As if she had been put through the wringer, nothing like the A-list celebrity that used her face like a weapon.

"You were supposed to change things, Bethany," Cassandra said, her voice sounding hollow, with a slight echo.

I tried to look at her eyes through the curtain of bangs, but it was hard. She kept darting around as if she didn't want me to see what was wrong with her.

Because there was something wrong. Her hand shook, and she kept pacing back and forth.

"Cassandra? What do you mean I was supposed to change things? Why are you here?" the love of my life asked, her voice so calm and controlled I knew there was nothing calm about her right then.

"You broke things up. You broke us. I thought we were together, Bethany. I thought we could both love him. Don't you understand that?"

Her words clicked something in my brain, and everything started to tie together, even if it still didn't make sense.

"You are the one emailing me?" Bethany asked, and I knew that she was going down the same path I was.

"Of course, I am. Haven't you noticed that I've always been there for you? Even before you found that stupid bitch, Lark, I was there for you. We had Dallas together. We are making it together. But you kept walking away. You kept thinking that we weren't good enough, but of course we are. He's sick and he is on drugs because of you. You're the one that did this to him."

Her voice began to ratchet up, and I moved, blocking Bethany's body with my own.

She tried to push me out of the way, but then Cassandra's arm went up, the gun facing us.

"I had to hurt someone to get in here. I couldn't let him see me. Because nobody does. Nobody sees *me*. But you did. Dallas did. I know the world hates us. I just wanted them to see us. That's why I sent the video. That's why I made sure the world saw how much Dallas loves you and you left him. Because we were together. We were always together. Why are you hurting him? Why are you hurting us?"

She was ranting and not making sense. She had done all this for some convoluted love or friendship or connection to Bethany?

There was seriously something wrong with

Cassandra Fox. But all I could think about was that she had a gun pointed at our faces. I wasn't sure I was fast enough to protect Bethany.

"Cassandra." Bethany let out a breath, and I heard tears in her voice. "Please put the gun down. We can talk about this."

"No. You hurt him. So I get to hurt you." Cassandra screamed and I moved. I moved quickly, pushing Bethany to the ground. Someone else was shouting and crying, and it could've been me. It could have been Bethany. It could have been Cassandra. I didn't know.

All I knew was that fire scorched up my arm, I was on the ground, my head slamming into the floor as I tried to cover Bethany with my body.

Something broke through the door, there was a shout. I wasn't sure what happened next.

Because the headache that had been building all day erupted, and there was nothing.

# Chapter Eighteen

Bethany

E ast held my hand as I sat in the waiting room, my heart still racing. I looked over at Everett's twin and studied his face.

While I knew intellectually that they looked nearly exactly alike, I could easily tell the two apart. All of the Wilders had dark hair and light eyes, chiseled jaws, and looked amazing in beards. But as East and Everett were identical twins, their only differences were from the lives they led.

East had a scar right below his eye, another on his jaw. While Everett's was near his temple. Everett smiled more and had a few more lines around his eyes and mouth. East scowled more, so the line between his brows was slightly more defined.

I thought East might have broken his nose at some point because there was a slight bump on his and not on Everett's.

East was also a little bit wider, all muscle. While Everett was all slender muscle, East had a little bit more bulk. Which made sense considering what his job was.

"Are you done studying me? Do you want to talk?"

I blushed and tried to pull away, but East held onto my hand.

"We're twins, identical. But we don't look alike anymore. He's the kind one. Of course, Elliot is the kindest of us all. But Everett is kinder than me."

I shook my head. "I think that he would say the same about you."

East snorted. "I don't think so. Are you okay here? The press hasn't caught wind of this yet, but they will. When they do, they will want to get photos of you. Even out here in the boondocks."

"I don't think the seventh-largest city in the country is the boondocks."

East snorted. "If you ask anybody outside of this area, that is what they're going to call it."

"I'm so tired of my family being here," Eli said from

the other side of the room, and I looked at Everett's brother, then reached out and squeezed his hand. Alexis paced along with Evan. Kendall, despite everybody's protests, sat in the waiting room with pillows all around her and her feet up. She was just fine, thank you very much. But one look from the nurse, and they took care of her, too.

Elliot sat with Maddie, the two going over things. I didn't know what it could be, but they spoke quietly in hushed tones.

Most of the family was here for Everett. Who would be fine. Everyone said he was going to be fine. And yet I couldn't believe it. Not until I held him in my arms.

But I wasn't next of kin, nor was I truly family. So I had to wait.

Thankfully the Wilders let me wait with them.

"Bethany?" Trace asked as he walked forward.

I sat up, my hands dropping from the Wilder brothers, and I looked over at my bodyguard. "Are you okay?"

Trace nodded and rubbed his shoulder. "I'm fine. Just asking about you."

I shrugged, then leaned back against the chair as he studied my face.

I didn't know what answers he was looking for, because I didn't have any.

He had broken through the door as we had locked it

behind us, and it was the fastest way in. I still wasn't sure how he had done that, but once he had seen Frank unconscious on the ground behind the house, he rushed in.

Cassandra Fox had gone through a possible psychotic break and had added fentanyl, alcohol, and other opioids to her system. She had been flailing for a long time, and nobody had known because she had always been so erratic in her persona.

She had broken into the house after knocking Frank out with a rock and had used that same rock to break a window in Everett's room.

Then she had waited for us.

She had waited in the woods, so nobody had seen her before the incident. And that was how she had been able to get through all of the Wilder security.

It still stunned me that it was Cassandra all this time. It'd been her with the notes and threats. Who thought somehow I was in a relationship with her and Dallas. That we were freely sharing him. I didn't know what she had wanted from her delusion, but she had broken along the way. And while later I would hope she was okay, I would hope she found that peace that I had spoken of, right then, I couldn't care. I wanted to, but I was too angry. Later, I would do more. But for now, I could only focus on getting Everett home.

Trace cleared his throat. "When you have time, I'd like to review the security with the Wilders. If you can. Bethany will be with this family for a long time, and I need to do a better job. We all do."

I blinked but Eli nodded. "Sounds like a plan. We're just supposed to be a wedding venue and winery. Supposed to have the security to keep threats out. But my family keeps getting hurt on my property. If I could somehow keep them safe, that would be wonderful."

"Don't blame yourself." Trace frowned. "This wasn't in your normal scope."

"People keep telling me that. And then Alexis gets hurt. Kendall. And now Everett. My family keeps getting hurt. I'm done. We're going to change things. The way we work. Because we were better when we were in active duty, and I'll be damned if I let my family get hurt again."

I nodded, knowing he was hurting. But before I could say anything, the doors opened, but it wasn't the nurse or doctor with Everett's updates. No, it was a woman with dark hair, bright eyes, and two large men beside her.

One I only recognized from a photo. But that was Eliza Wilder Montgomery and her husband, Beckett.

And the other man?

He was a shadow.

Elijah came forward, looking haggard, dark circles under his eyes. He looked exhausted, and all I wanted to do was reach up and hug him, but I knew if I did, we'd all break. He didn't look welcome to the idea of touch, so I didn't. But this had to be breaking him. It was all so much, and I was surprised he was even there.

"Elijah picked us up from the airport. We're here." Eliza ran into Eli's arms, and he hugged his baby sister as everyone began speaking at once, hugging each other as they did.

I looked over at Maddie, who just shook her head, feeling as lost as I did. They had all been through so much together and only wanted Everett to be okay. I knew that nothing was ever going to be the same.

I told myself that when I had found Dallas cheating on me. And then again when I had found Everett at the resort. I knew things were forever altered the moment I fell for him again and he had done the same.

I told myself that my path had forever changed course when Cassandra and Dallas had shared the recording. And then again when Everett and I fought for each other.

Now Everett was hurt, and I wasn't there with him. But I would never let him go again.

We would find a way to make this work. Because we had fought through hell once, and we would do it again.

I just needed him to be okay.

I didn't know what would happen next. I didn't know how we would blend our two lives together, but as I saw his family come together as one, I knew I wanted to be part of this. I knew I would find a way to make that happen.

"Bethany?"

I looked up as Eliza came forward, her arms outstretched. "I thought it would be nice if we met in person."

I stood up and found myself being hugged by Eliza, her arms tight.

"I would say it's good to meet you, but I kind of wish it was under better circumstances," I said as Eliza wiped her tears.

I hadn't cried yet. I couldn't, not until I saw him. He had hit his head so hard when he had pushed me down to save my life. Then there had been so much blood.

I just needed him to be here. So I could hold him. And wrap him in cotton wool so he would be safe.

"Well, we met. As soon as my brother is done playing hero, I can hug him. We can all sit down and eat some comfort food."

"I would help with that, but they're not letting me cook."

We all turned to see Kendall, her hands over her belly. "Oh I'm fine over here. Just feeling ignored."

She was fluttering her eyelashes, and I knew she was trying to cut the tension. For that, I was grateful.

Eliza went right over to Kendall, kissed her sister-in-law square on the mouth, and then kissed her belly. "I'm so excited. Hello, babies."

"Where's your baby?" Eli asked softly. "Did you bring Lexington?"

Eliza nodded. "I did. He is currently with my brother-in-law and his husband."

Beckett cleared his throat. "Archer and Killian flew with us so they can take care of Lexington when we were otherwise occupied and check on the family. You know how they love you Wilders."

I looked between all of them, my throat tight. "So many connections. I'm glad that you guys have each other."

"You have us now, too," Elliot said as he hugged me tightly.

I nodded, wiping tears from my gaze. When the doctor walked in, I swallowed hard, the room getting suddenly quiet.

"Is this the family for Everett Wilder?" the doctor asked. I wasn't surprised by the look of shock on his face. There were a lot of us, and the Wilders, as well as

Trace and Beckett, were all big. There was no hiding them.

We also were in a special room, rather than the main waiting room, because of me. While on any other day, that might make me feel a little rude for using my privilege, right then, all that mattered was that nobody was going to try to get photos of me. The Wilders would be able to breathe and be safe without my world crashing into theirs once again.

"We are Everett's family," Eli answered. "Can we see him?"

The doctor once again looked around at everyone, saw me, and his eyes widened. He did do a good job of clearing his throat and pretending that he hadn't recognized me. I was grateful because I still wasn't used to it even though it was my life.

"All of you are family?" the doctor asked, clearly not believing Eli.

"We are all family," East growled, sounding more like the East I had come to know.

"Okay then. You can go in the back soon in groups of two. Visiting hours end at six, though, so you don't have that much time. Your brother has allowed me to share this information with his family. Everett will be fine. It was a graze to his arm, so we dealt with it easily. We took a bit longer because of his TBI, and his doctors were in the hospital so they wanted to check for signs of concussion from the fall." He held up his hand, as everybody spoke at once. Thankfully, everybody quieted down. "There are no signs of concussion. He will be able to go home soon. We will not keep him overnight, but it will be a few hours before he can leave. Now, you guys get to decide amongst yourselves who gets to see him first."

I was grateful for his humor because it cut the tension quickly.

Before I could blink, though, everybody was pushing me towards the front, with Elijah being the strongest proponent.

"No, you should go first. I'll go last. Don't worry. I'm okay."

"That's a damn lie," Elijah growled. "Go see him. We'll all see you either tonight or tomorrow. Because he's coming home. Don't take this for granted, Bethany. One blink, and it could have been different. So go in there and tell him we love him. Don't wait."

And with that, he turned on his heel and walked out of the room, the swinging doors squeaking behind him.

Eliza pressed her lips together before she followed him, her husband and Elliot right behind her. East grabbed my hand and tugged me down the hall, ignoring my protests, but I was grateful for it. Because I didn't want to wait.

And then we were there outside his room, and I swallowed hard, wondering what I would say.

"I'll wait out here. You go see him first."

The Wilders were making me crazy. "I don't understand any of you. Shouldn't you be in there?"

"The only person that he wants to see right now is you. So let that happen, and we will be right behind you. Our family needs this. We need you."

"But I'm the reason he's here." That's when the reality of the situation hit me. Because these people were here, in the hospital, and Everett was hurt because of me. This was on me. There was no denying that. No matter what the Wilders said.

"I'm going to let my brother beat your ass for that. Because you don't get to blame yourself for this. If he doesn't get mad at you for that statement, I'm blaming the injury. But not you, now, go in there." He practically pushed me to the door, and then Everett was there, looking at me, his brows raised.

He had a bandage on his arm, and it was in a sling, but he looked fine. As if he hadn't been shot earlier. My knees went weak at that thought, and I opened my mouth to say something, to say anything, but I could only gasp.

"Everett?"

I had been so strong. Or at least I tried to be. I had rolled my shoulders back. I had talked to the authorities. I had done everything to be strong. But one look at him, and I couldn't hold back.

I broke down into tears, and Everett cursed.

"Damn it. Now I need to get out of this bed, and that nurse is going to come in and beat me." He grumbled under his breath as I heard the bed creak. I moved quickly, trying to force him back down.

"Don't you dare, Everett Wilder. You do not move. You got shot because of me. If I'm going to cry, I will. You just have to get over it."

"I love your bedside manner. You are working hard at it."

"Why did you push me out of the way? You got hurt because of me."

Everett scowled. "No, I got hurt because a woman was self-medicating and hurting herself and took it out on you. I stood in the way, so you didn't get harmed, but that wasn't on either one of us."

"I can't believe Cassandra was behind all of this."

Everett shook his head and winced. "I can't believe that either, but the authorities apparently are piecing everything together from our statements and her own evidence. Cassandra Fox needs help. And she'll get it.

But right now, I don't care about her. I only care about you. Are you okay, Bethany? And why aren't you touching me?"

I swallowed hard, then reached out, touching his hand gingerly.

He cursed again and gripped my hand tight. "I want you in bed with me."

I blushed and wiped my eyes. "You say that all the time, but right now I'm not getting in that bed with you. You are in a sling. They were checking you for a concussion. After your brain injury? Do you think that's a bad idea?"

"Of course, it's a bad idea, so I want to do it."

"Stop trying to make me laugh."

"Is it working?" he asked softly.

"I don't know. I was so scared. Your family is here. Everyone came. Your sister and brother-in-law. Apparently there are two more from her family here that I don't really know how they're related. But they're here, they brought babies, and everyone's talking. Even Elijah showed up for a minute."

Pain crossed Everett's features that had nothing to do with the gunshot wound. "Damn it. Is he still here?"

I shook my head. "No, but others went after him."

"He has enough on his plate without worrying about me. He's always worrying about us."

"See, you just need to get healthy so we can worry about him together."

"I like the sound of that. Together. You're not going to leave me because of this? Because damn it, Bethany. That would hurt me more than any gunshot wound."

"Now you are just talking crap."

"We'll make this work. You don't get to blame yourself for what happened."

"I brought her into your life." My heart ached, the guilt overriding everything in that moment.

"No. She brought herself into the situation. She had this fictional idea of who you were. Of what you were. That is on her. And that is something she will have to deal with when she sobers up. That has nothing to do with us."

I ran my hands through my hair as I looked down at him. "The media storm is going to be insane. They are going to figure out everything. About her. About us. Everything."

"And we'll weather that storm. We will, because you're not leaving me over this. I love you, Bethany. I said to the ends of the earth, and I meant it. I didn't realize you be quite so close about literal end right now, but I'm still here. You don't get to leave now. You're stuck with me. All of us Wilders."

"Damn straight," East said through the door, and I laughed.

"You weren't supposed to be listening!" I called out.

East walked in, shaking his head. "I never actually promised that. I just said you could come in first. We have to move this along, because there is a line waiting to get in here." East winked at me and scowled down at his twin.

"You okay?"

"I will be. What about you?"

"I didn't get the twin tingling or anything like that. So I guess that's something."

I looked between them, tears still rolling down my cheeks. "You guys are nothing alike and yet the same person. I have no idea how that works," I said with a laugh.

"True enough," they both said simultaneously, then grinned.

"Don't get shot again," East warned.

"I'll do my best. Now, let me kiss my woman, and I guess see the rest of the family."

"Sounds like a plan. I'll get them. Keep on kissing." East walked out then, and I shook my head, feeling like I was struggling to keep up.

"I don't get the two of you."

"You don't have to. Now, kiss me, woman."

"If you insist."

I pressed my lips to his cheek, and he growled.

"Damn it. A real kiss. And then maybe I'll let you go. But only for the evening because I'm never really letting you go. Ever."

I smiled softly, my heart breaking and melting and growing all at once. I pressed my lips to his, soft, sweet, with every emotion pulling through.

"I'm not letting you go either. But please, don't throw yourself in front of a bullet for me again."

"I would do anything for you, Bethany," Everett said, all serious now. "Everything. Just like I know you would do the same for me. I know it's not going to be easy. That's okay. Because we will have each other. Now, hold me. I have a boo-boo."

I threw my head back and laughed as other Wilders piled in, completely ignoring the orders from the nurse. I knew I was once again in trouble.

But I loved this wild side of my Wilder.

And I would prove every day that I earned him.

That I was worth him.

That we were so much more together than we ever had been apart.

# Chapter Nineteen

### Everett

In the months since the shooting, healing hadn't come easy, but being with Bethany? Far easier than the world might've thought. I smiled as I looked down at the woman that I loved, the woman that I would one day make mine in truth. She looked up at me, a questioning look in her gaze.

"What's that look for?"

"Just thinking that I love you."

"You're thinking that you do, or you do? Because now you're confusing me."

I grumbled, frowning. "Now you are just confusing me."

"Sorry. I can't help it. I'm so glad your sister could come down just to see us for a while. I know it's been hard because we've been back and forth between here and LA, but I so love being with you and everyone else."

"I'm glad that she could make it. And now that the twins are born, it's nice to have an extra pair of hands."

She rolled her eyes. "Like those babies have ever been set down. Every time I look around, there's another Wilder holding a bundle of adorable joy, and my ovaries scream."

I swallowed hard. "If you want, we can go practice trying to make a baby. Purely to help you out."

Lark came forward with a roll of her eyes. "That wasn't even a smooth move."

Bethany wrapped her arm around her best friend and squeezed tight. "He tries. But I'm sure we'll practice, Everett."

Lark made a gagging noise. "Just not when I'm in the room. Again."

"You walked into the living room. I don't see how that's my fault," Bethany laughed.

"It was totally your fault," Lark put in. "Now. If you two are done being adorably disgusting, we have cake to eat."

"Did someone say cake?" I asked, licking my lips.

"You just ate two helpings of dinner. Now you want cake?"

"Of course. Why not cake?" I scoffed.

"You confuse me. But I love you."

"You know you want cake too."

"Possibly. I can't help it."

We smiled at each other before reality set in. "Are you all packed up for the return trip?" I asked.

She nodded, searching my gaze. "And I'll see you in five days."

"That's not that long. We can make it."

Bethany lived with me while we were down here in San Antonio, and I lived with her at her place in LA. When she was on location, I went there. Eventually, I would build a place, as my brothers had done, but I wanted Bethany to be the one to help me choose what we had. After all, I wasn't letting her go, so she would make the decisions.

It wasn't easy. We didn't get to see each other every day like most couples. But we did our best. We always made sure we never went more than five days without seeing each other, even if it meant complicated schedules. But I was lucky. My job allowed me to do that, and my family made sure that it happened as well.

One day things would slow down, but right now

Bethany was shooting a movie and that was strenuous on her and her time. So I was the one who traveled more. When she had more downtime, she would travel more to me. Compromise was our relationship, and we made it work.

I didn't know exactly what the future held for us beyond the fact that one day I would make her my wife. But first, we wanted to take some time. Just for us. So we weren't rushing into anything. It felt like our relationship had already been rushed enough.

The media would always be around. They would always want to know more of us. They would always take more than we allowed. But we also had each other. No matter what happened, we made things work.

I'd almost lost her multiple times. Just like I had lost part of myself.

But now we were finding it again, and that was all that mattered.

We went to the dessert table, as Lark and Bethany each got themselves cake and handed me a slice. I smiled down at them, then at my family.

Most of us were here, a family dinner that we tried to do once a week even if I wasn't here. Video calling into family dinner was weird, but we were trying. Eliza did it, after all, when she was up at her house in Colorado.

We had spent far too much time apart for us to change things now.

The only person that wasn't here was a jagged wound that I didn't know would heal.

But Elijah didn't want to be near us. He didn't want to be near anyone.

And as I remembered Bethany's scream when I had nearly lost her, I didn't blame him.

He came to work every day. He did his duty. And then he went home. We each took turns taking care of him. I didn't know how we could fix that. How we could make things better.

I didn't even know if we could make it better.

But we would be here when he needed us.

Because he hadn't given up on me when I felt lost.

So I would never give up on him.

"Serious thoughts?" Bethany asked.

I smiled down at her. "Just a little."

"Do you want to talk about it?"

"When we get home. Right now, just be here. And the cake."

She used her fork to take off a bite and stuck it in my mouth. I grinned around the tines of the fork, shaking my head when she slid the fork out of my mouth.

I swallowed, the decadent cream cheese frosting my favorite. "Well, that's the best cake ever."

"You're welcome," Kendall called out from the couch, a baby in her arm. East had the other baby as Evan scowled, trying to take the baby from my twin.

I laughed, since the babies were constantly being traded around, Eliza's Lexington was the same.

I still couldn't believe that this was our life. That these angry brothers of mine, the ones that had been through hell and back, injured, losing parts of our souls along the way, had somehow become family men. At least some of us.

We would find a way, too.

We were growing as a family, and I was so damn blessed that I didn't want anyone else to feel as lost as I had before.

I looked down at Bethany and smiled. "I'm so damn glad that you accosted me on my porch."

She rolled her eyes as Lark laughed into her cake.

"This is my favorite story," Lark put in.

"Yes, yelling at a man with a headache who later passes out is totally your favorite story."

"I might have already put it into a song."

"Let me hear it?" I asked, and Lark just winked.

"One day."

"Well, I'm glad I so-called accosted you as well. I mean, who could ever forget about me." She fluttered her eyelashes, and I wrapped my arm around her shoulders, tilted her head back, and kissed her hard.

People cheered or scoffed, depending on which brother it was, and I just grinned against her mouth.

"I love you."

"I love you too. Then let me have my cake."

I threw my head back and laughed and figured that things might not be perfect, but they were ours. Finally.

I had the woman of my dreams. The woman of my past. The woman of my forgotten memories.

This was only the start of our path. After all, we were only a beginning.

# Chapter Twenty

Maddie

I needed to clear my head. To go on a walk, to just breathe. Nothing had seemed right in weeks, and I wasn't sure if it would feel right again. Why did everything hurt?

Oh, I knew why everything hurt. Because guilt, shame, grief, sorrow, and hope in the absence of everything else twisted like a gnarled knot of thorns within my heart.

"Good, you're here," Alexis stated as she held up her tablet. "Can you take a look at this for me?"

I lifted my chin and smiled. "Always. What is it?"

"It's a contract I have coming up with a potential bride, but I want you to take a look at it."

I frowned. "Why would you need me to do that? This is your expertise. Elliot's too, honestly."

"Because they are from a former wine tour party that came in a couple of weeks ago and were *particular*."

The way she said particular reminded me exactly who she was talking about. That tour had been a pain and made my head hurt just thinking about it.

I grimaced. "Oh. So she got her engagement then," I said after a while.

"She did. And she's happy. But this wedding will be bigger than anything we've done, including our celebrity weddings. And since you worked with them before on contracts with the tour and the winery, I thought you could go over it with me to ensure I don't miss anything. Not that I think I did, and not that I think any of the Wilders did. But, I don't know, I'm nervous."

Alexis bounced from foot to foot, something that she rarely did. Alexis was calm, collected, and knew what she wanted. I remembered this tour, and how particular they were.

And the fact that their families were connected to some of the biggest oil, money, and real estate moguls in the state.

If we did well on this, it could be big for the

Wilders. If we screwed it up, there would be no coming back from that. At least not easily.

"I will totally take a look at it. Do you want it right now? I was about to go for a walk." I rubbed my temple, not meaning to, and she caught the gesture.

"Oh, we have a couple of days. I just wanted to ask. But take your time. Do you need something for your head?" She gave me a worried look.

I shook my head. "I'm fine. It's just a normal headache."

Not exactly, but I wasn't quite sure telling her that I felt heartsick over something I couldn't change would help. She knew what I felt. She had seen it all over my face the first time she met me. She was also feeling some of the same things I did.

Because we all missed Joy.

I still couldn't believe that she was gone. That with everything the Wilders and all of their friends had gone through; this was what might break us.

I couldn't think so fatalistically, but it was hard not to when my heart was breaking thinking about losing our friend.

It didn't matter that at one point, I had fashioned myself in love with Joy's boyfriend. They hadn't been together when I had fallen for him, and I had quickly suppressed and ignored my feelings, to the point that they weren't even there anymore once I realized that the two of them were serious.

Joy hadn't had an inkling of what I'd once wanted. I would never have gone after the man she'd loved, and I wouldn't ever want that now. But the guilt that I had coveted her boyfriend, even if she hadn't known, and even if it had been before we had even met, ate at me.

I needed to go for a walk to clear my head.

Because it was hard working for the Wilders, to be here day in and day out, to be near this family that was hurting, my friends. To be near *him*.

Alexis hugged me without saying a word and then left me alone in my office, the ping on my own tablet telling me she had forwarded the contract to me.

While I knew Alexis would like me to look through things for her, I also knew that wasn't the reason she'd come here. She had wanted to check on me. Which we kept doing for each other.

Because one of our friends was dead. Just like that, snuffed out of existence, and nobody knew what to do about it.

Nobody knew what to do to help grieve, let alone help Elijah.

A bitter taste coated my tongue as I thought of him, but I pushed those thoughts out of my mind. They wouldn't help anyone. They would just make things harder. So I slid my phone into my pocket, as well as a walkie-talkie just in case I made it to a place that didn't have the greatest service, and made my way outside.

I loved this area of Wilder Wines and their properties. The vines were in the east, but I could walk through the foothills, the small little so-called mountains of the San Antonio area. Nothing like the Rockies or Appalachians or Cascades. But still beautiful.

It was a different kind of beauty, one that had called to me my entire life.

And yet they hurt me because all I could do was think about the fact that Joy would never see them again.

She was gone in a blink.

And everything hurt.

Thankful that I had grabbed my metal water canister, I took a big gulp and made my way through the trees and small hills that were on the property.

The sun wasn't directly overhead, but it was still hot. I wiped my brow, wondering exactly why I was taking this walk now. I could've done it at any other time, but I needed a moment for myself. I needed to breathe. I circled a copse of trees, my legs straining as I continued to climb up the hill. I wouldn't say it was a mountain, but my thighs felt like it was.

The sun shone on my face, the sky full of cedar and

oak, my allergies running rampant. I ignored them, knowing I would pay for this later.

I just needed this moment.

When I turned the corner around the rock face, I nearly tripped over my feet, my heart thudding in my chest, my breath nearly coming in pants. I don't know why I expected anything different.

Of course, *he* would be here.

At my North Star, the place where I was headed, to find space. Of course, he would be the one I would be drawn to even if I told myself it didn't make any sense. Because he hadn't been mine before, and I could never let him be mine now.

Elijah stood at the edge of the cliff, where it dropped quickly. It wasn't the best place to stand, and he was past the ropes now, past the route that was safe. We were still on Wilder property, but nobody really came out here. There were so many other things to do on Wilder land, that most people never made it out here. And yet, here Elijah was.

At my touchstone.

I was his friend, nothing more. Because I saw his love for Joy, and I had never had anything like that. Not with him, not with anyone. I knew who his true happiness had been with, and it was never with me.

I had come to terms with that a long time ago. Only,

seeing him there, in pain, standing as he stared down into the abyss, I had to wonder what he was supposed to do now.

"I should've known you would be here," he said after a moment. His voice was rough, harsh. I knew he didn't mean it to lash out at me. I knew he was broken inside, jagged shards of the man that he was.

Elijah was slick in a suit, the man who could smile and get his way. He was happy, and he did everything with a purpose. His job hadn't sent him around the world into dangerous areas the way that his brothers' had. His job in the Air Force had been safer. At least in my mind. But he had always watched his brothers come home broken.

And now he was the one breaking, and there was nothing I could do.

"I came here for a moment of peace. I didn't realize you would be here. I didn't mean to intrude on your privacy. I'm sorry. I can go." I sputtered the words, trying to figure out what to say. Instead, he gave a rough laugh.

"What am I supposed to do now, Maddie?"

I swallowed hard and told myself not to cry. He needed someone stronger than that. I couldn't be the one that cried first.

I moved so I stood next to him but still gave him

space. So he wouldn't think I was horning in on his moments.

"I don't know, Elijah. Your family is here. You don't have to do it alone."

In that moment, I knew I had said the wrong things. Because being alone didn't mean not being surrounded by people.

He gave a hollow laugh and then lifted a black velvet box out of his pocket. I sucked in a harsh breath as tears stung my eyes and I swallowed hard. He opened up the lid, a gleaming sapphire solitaire sat on black velvet, stunning, unique, and *Joy*.

"I thought I was finally making peace. Finding my path. I thought she was the one I would come home to. I was wrong." At that, he looked directly into my eyes. It felt like he was wrapping around my soul, knew exactly who I was, and every thought I'd ever had before about him. I felt alone, bare. "I'm not making that mistake again, Maddie," he said in a harsh tone.

And before I could say anything to that, he crumbled. There was no other word for it. He crumbled and fell to his knees as heart-wrenching sobs escaped him. It was as if a phoenix broke, burned to an ember as it wailed its sorrow.

Elijah cried. Something I had never seen him do.

I stood beside him, my hand on his shoulder, his warmth searing my ice-cold skin.

In looking at him, I knew the truth. Love broke you.

Neither one of us would ever be the same again. Nor should we.

We would never fall. He would never be mine. I knew this before. As I watched him break, I knew I never wanted him to be mine.

I never wanted that pain. I never wanted Elijah to feel anything like that again.

So I held him, knowing that this was the end. An end.

With no beginning.

# Bonus Epilogue

### Everett

I turned the corner, smashed my forehead into a low arch, and cursed under my breath, backing up a few steps.

I had never thought the expression "seeing stars" was true until this moment. Which was saying something, considering everything my brain had gone through.

"Everett! Are you okay? Oh my God."

Bethany ran towards me, the sounds of her flip-flops on the marble floors echoing through her LA home.

Well, I guess *our* LA home.

It was still odd to think that we had moved in together, and had not one, but two places. But this was the love of my life, and I was learning how to navigate the seas of movie-stardom. Even as long as we'd been together, we were learning.

Not that I was ever going to figure out that path entirely.

"I'm fine," I said, rubbing my forehead. "Who thought that building low arches in LA was smart?"

Bethany winced. "I know. When I'm in my stilettos, sometimes I have to duck so I don't brush my hair against the bottom of it. I don't usually go this way for that reason. I'm sorry." She cupped my cheeks, met my gaze, and I knew she was making sure I didn't have a concussion. Then I bent low when she went up to her tiptoes and breathed in a sigh of relief as the softness of her lips brushed against my skin.

"I'm okay. I promise. If you could help with those flying birds around my head, that'd be great." The panic in her gaze made me curse again, and I winced. "I'm sorry, babe. I didn't mean that. I'm fine. I'm just an idiot." I frowned. "You have friends over here, friends from your movies. And they're all way taller than me."

"I sort of put this chaise lounge in front of it, so

people come over here without knocking their heads into things. We're going to need to do some remodeling if we're going to keep the house. It's been on my list. I just haven't gotten to it yet."

She dropped her hands from my face, so I wrapped my arms around her waist, bringing her close. Her breasts pressed against my chest, and I grinned wickedly.

She rolled her eyes, even as she ground against me slightly.

"I thought you had work to do, Wilder."

"There are things we could do before I check my email. I mean, where is that chaise lounge? I'm sure I can bend you over it." I smacked her lightly on the ass, and she let out a groan before wiggling. My dick stood at attention. I pressed my lips together, doing my best not to actually fulfill that promise.

"You are a temptation."

"So says the man who is holding me tight to his cock." She rolled her eyes, and I squeezed her slightly before letting her go.

"Okay, let me go get back to work. I know the company can't run without me. They are probably running around all lost, searching for me, calling out my name."

She rolled her eyes again. "Yes. That's exactly what they're doing. It's not like you haven't been working here for hours a day, constantly at their beck and call because it is your job and you love them."

I frowned. "Is that okay? Is this working out?"

Considering we were still working out this whole living together in multiple places around the world thing, I wasn't sure what I wanted the answer to be.

I loved Bethany. I loved her smile, her kindness, her brain. I loved everything about her. But I was also fully aware that while we both were the number ones in each other's lives, we each had responsibilities that sometimes took us away from the other.

We were going to make it work. We were open about it, and were doing everything possible to ensure that we didn't screw this up.

But no relationship was easy, and ours was a different kind of difficult than most.

"Of course, this is working out, Everett." She slapped playfully at my chest. "What takes a little bit of getting used to is sharing a house, because I've never lived with anyone before. But I love waking up next to you. Even if you're still long asleep after I leave."

"It's not my fault that you sometimes have a 3 a.m. wake-up call. It's a little scary."

I shuddered to think about it, and she laughed. "You get used to it. And you're the best because you always make sure that I get to sleep early, even if it's a little bit earlier than I wanted."

"I'm figuring out my own timetable, too. I can work anywhere, most of the time. With technology, I can video chat with my family, and I do have emails and phone calls. And you are being amazing and coming out to Texas with me when you don't have to be out here or on another shoot."

"We're heading out to Texas tomorrow. And we're all packed, so we can get some work done today before we leave, and then we have a month there. I have those scripts to read and a few other business tasks that can be done from anywhere before I have my shoot."

She cringed, but I pushed her back softly, cupped her face, and kissed her on the cheek.

"And you will go out on your own for a bit, and I will come to visit you. We'll make this work. Not everybody has a 9-to-5 job. We sure don't. So, we just have to make compromises. And the fact that I'm able to come out with you is a blessing."

She crossed her eyes at me and laughed. "You know, I thought I was the one reassuring you. But here you are, doing it for me."

I shrugged and kissed her again.

"Because I love you. And yes, I'm worried that I'm screwing up your life. You are the best thing that's ever happened to me. I'm not going to risk messing it up."

Her eyes filled with tears before she quickly blinked them away. "You say the sweetest things, Everett. How do you do that?"

I beamed. "It's natural talent. I'm just that good."

She laughed, and I tried not to take offense at that.

"Are you sure you're all packed?"

"Totally. I've gotten good at it."

"You think we should take the Oscar?" I asked, looking over her head into her new office. She had removed everything from her old office, a memory she didn't want to deal with. And in doing so, she had the perfect space for her new Academy award. The ceremony and everything leading up to it had been insane. I still wasn't sure how I had even gotten through it. She had been a trooper, a brilliant star who could do anything. She had weathered through the storm of news media and campaigning. She had done brilliantly.

And it didn't matter that we had been in our relationship for months, that our moving back and forth wasn't anything new, the worry that etched in our bones from it still came, but my pride in her never wavered.

I loved her and everything she represented.

"I guess if you want to bring me Oscar, I think it would look better with the Wilders anyway. That way, he's not out here in LA all alone."

I kissed her again. "I love you, Bethany Cole."

"I love you too, Everett Wilder." She gave me an odd look, and I realized that I sounded a little odd, a little formal.

That's when I knew that all plans of me standing on a hilltop, with the moon above us didn't really need to happen. Nor did standing on a beach with the waves crashing around us.

No setting would be perfect, because they all were as long as I was with her.

I swallowed hard and looked at her and hoped I was doing the right thing.

When I went to one knee, Bethany's eyes widened and her hands covered her mouth.

"Everett."

"I found you when I wasn't expecting you. You found me when we both needed each other the most. I will forever wish for the days that we could have had, but in the end, we have each other now. I will weather whatever storm comes at us, because I know we will do it together. It took a long time for me to find the path to you, but here we are, on the only path worth taking. I will follow you to the ends of the earth, be with you no matter where you go. To watch the woman you are shine and grow into the goddess that you are becoming. I adore you, Bethany Cole. I love you. And I know it won't be easy, but nothing worth forever is. Will you make me the happiest man in the world and be my wife?" I paused. "Not that I'm being possessive, but I'm really being possessive right now," I said with a laugh.

At that, knowing I had probably just ruined the end of my proposal, Bethany threw her head back and laughed.

"Well, I don't know if that was exactly what I was going for," I said, a little nervous, even though I was laughing with her.

She went to her knees and wrapped her arms around my neck. "I love you so much, Everett. Of course, I'll marry you. You're going to be stuck with me now. Because we will be the 'It Couple,' just like we are now, but we will be so for everyone. And yet, only for us. Because that's all that matters. I love you so much. And I cannot wait to be a Wilder."

She kissed me hard on the mouth, and I smiled.

"You're really going to change your name?"

"Legally, yes. I want to be Bethany Wilder. I'll be

Bethany Cole for my job, but at home? I'm all yours. All Wilder."

I kissed her hard. "I love you. And that sounds like a damn good time."

I slid the antique twenties era ring on her finger, knowing it might not be the biggest ring out there, especially not in her circuit, but it was something that I had found, something I could afford. She just smiled at me, then kissed me again.

"I can't wait to be your wife."

"I can't wait to be yours," I whispered

"You already are."

We kissed again, laughing as we rolled around on the floor.

I had my Hollywood ending, and the credits would roll, but all that mattered was I had the one woman I hadn't thought I needed. The one woman who would always be there.

I would spend the rest of my days proving that I deserved her.

And we would follow the path we had found together.

One achingly different and worthwhile step at a time.

\*\*\*

# NEXT IN THE WILDER BROTHERS SERIES:
## Elijah and Maddie find their way in
## COMING HOME FOR US.

# A Note from Carrie Ann Ryan

Thank you so much for reading **THE PATH TO YOU.**

I've always wanted to write an opposites attract romance with a celebrity finding her way. They were some of my favorite kinds of books growing up, but finding a way to make it work with the Wilders was too much fun, even when I cried a bit.

Everett and Bethany's romance was one about finding your path even when it twists on you. And the Wilders aren't going anyway any time soon.

I also fell in love with a side character and I didn't meant to. So Trace? You might have to wait for me a bit because I have and idea....

And we're just getting started with the Wilder Brothers.

Elijah and Maddie's romance is...well. Healing needs to take place and their romance is one of the sweetest things I've ever written. I hope you love it as much as I do.

## The Wilder Brothers Series:

## NEXT IN THE WILDER BROTHERS SERIES:
### Elijah and Maddie find their way in COMING HOME FOR US.

If you want to make sure you know what's coming next from me, you can sign up for my newsletter at www. CarrieAnnRyan.com; follow me on twitter at @CarrieAnnRyan, or like my Facebook page. I also have a Facebook Fan Club where we have trivia, chats, and other goodies. You guys are the reason I get to do what I do and I thank you.

Make sure you're signed up for my MAILING LIST so

you can know when the next releases are available as well as find giveaways and FREE READS.

Happy Reading!

# Also from Carrie Ann Ryan

**The Montgomery Ink Legacy Series:**

**The Wilder Brothers Series:**

**The Aspen Pack Series:**

Book 1: Etched in Honor

Book 2: Hunted in Darkness

Book 3: Mated in Chaos

Book 4: Harbored in Silence

Book 5: Marked in Flames

## The Montgomery Ink: Fort Collins Series:

Book 1: Inked Persuasion

Book 2: Inked Obsession

Book 3: Inked Devotion

Book 3.5: Nothing But Ink

Book 4: Inked Craving

Book 5: Inked Temptation

## The Montgomery Ink: Boulder Series:

Book 1: Wrapped in Ink

Book 2: Sated in Ink

Book 3: Embraced in Ink

Book 3: Moments in Ink

Book 4: Seduced in Ink

Book 4.5: Captured in Ink

Book 4.7: Inked Fantasy

Book 4.8: A Very Montgomery Christmas

## Montgomery Ink: Colorado Springs

Book 1: Fallen Ink

## The Whiskey and Lies Series:

Book 1: Whiskey Secrets

Book 2: Whiskey Reveals

Book 3: Whiskey Undone

## The Gallagher Brothers Series:

Book 1: Love Restored

Book 2: Passion Restored

Book 3: Hope Restored

## The Ravenwood Coven Series:

Book 1: Dawn Unearthed

Book 2: Dusk Unveiled

Book 3: Evernight Unleashed

## The Talon Pack:

Book 1: Tattered Loyalties

Book 2: An Alpha's Choice

Book 3: Mated in Mist

Book 4: Wolf Betrayed

Book 5: Fractured Silence

Book 6: Destiny Disgraced

Book 7: Eternal Mourning

Book 8: Strength Enduring

Book 9: Forever Broken

Book 10: Mated in Darkness

## Holiday, Montana Series:

## The Branded Pack Series:
## (Written with Alexandra Ivy)

# About the Author

Carrie Ann Ryan is the New York Times and USA Today bestselling author of contemporary, paranormal, and young adult romance. Her works include the Montgomery Ink, Redwood Pack, Fractured Connections, and Elements of Five series, which have sold over 3.0 million books worldwide. She started writing while in graduate school for her advanced degree in chemistry and hasn't stopped since. Carrie Ann has written over seventy-five novels and novellas with more in the works. When she's not losing herself in her emotional and action-packed worlds, she's reading as much as she can while wrangling her clowder of cats who have more followers than she does.

www.CarrieAnnRyan.com

www.ingramcontent.com/pod-product-compliance
Lightning Source LLC
Chambersburg PA
CBHW011449100726
47899CB00010BB/3216